People of the Flow

Ben H. Gagnon

Beacon Publishing Group
P.O. Box 41573 Charleston, S.C. 29423
800.817.8480| beaconpublishinggroup.com

Publisher's catalog available by request.

ISBN-13: 978-1-949472-64-6

ISBN-10: 1-949472-64-7

Published in 2019. New York, NY 10001.

First Edition. Printed in the USA

Christian Sia – 5 Stars

"In a work filled with imagination, Ben H. Gagnon creates a story that leaves readers feeling as though they just woke up from a dream. The prose is fluid and filled with insightful passages and powerful imagery. The novel stands alone in its originality and its power to entertain readers. A beautiful read, indeed."

Deborah Lloyd – 5 stars

"There are many compelling aspects to this book ... How the author connects all of this in one novel is truly masterful! ... a must-read for those who love Irish history or traditional religions."

Romuald Dzemo – 5 Stars

" A novel with a powerful international setting and strong spiritual undertones ... [the protagonist] follows a path that is filled with mystery and wonder. The writing is gorgeous and lyrical .... The images that flood the mind of the reader allow them glimpses of Ireland. Filled with compelling and memorable characters, it is cunningly plotted and beautifully written."

K.C. Finn – 5 Stars

"John is a character whose knowledge and intuition you feel you can trust ... leading you through a fascinating mystery and discovery process that keeps you turning the pages.The novel's conclusion is a striking success, leaving the reader with many lingering thoughts about the differences between myth and fact ... a highly recommended read."

Chapter One

Townland of Disert, County Cork, Ireland, April 3, 1893

Drifting in the darkness, low over the hills and pastures, the heavy fog lit up in a flash. The off-shore storm grumbled. Atop a white, clapboard house at the base of a steep hill, a swan-shaped vane turned in the wind, swinging east, then north.

Little fingers pulled on a rope that lowered the stairs to the attic. The wooden steps barely creaked under her bare feet. Nessa went to a small window in the front of the attic and opened it. The mist came in. She took a green leather book from her little rocking chair, held it to her chest and sat down, slowly moving forward and backward, staring into the fog. In the bedroom below, Mary Ó Dálaigh woke. She shook her husband.

"There's a noise."

"Where?" Gerald Ó Dálaigh's ribs ached from being kicked by a pony during his veterinary rounds the day before.

"Shh," said Mary.

They both heard the sound of creaking boards above. Venturing into the hallway, Gerald saw the attic stairs pulled down. He forgot the pain and climbed into the attic, candle in hand. Mary followed. In a flash of yellowish-green light, Gerald saw Nessa rocking back and forth below the open window. Rain was splashing on the windowsill.

"Nessa?" he called. There was no reply. "Nessa!" Still nothing.

"Jesus, Mary and Joseph!" whispered Mary, crossing herself. Gerald squatted down in front of Nessa, but she didn't stop rocking, or clasping the book.

"Nessa darlin'," he whispered. She stared at the fog. Every few seconds, it lit up with distant lightning. "What are you doin' here by the window?"

Nessa's breathing was slow and even. Her orange hair was damp. Gerald closed the window and took her in his arms.

"She's never done this," said Mary. "Goin' into the attic."

"Get some towels, Mary," said Gerald. "I'll take her back to her room." With Nessa quiet in his arms, he carefully made his way down the steps. He was putting her back in bed when Mary returned with a towel, then retreated to the doorway.

"She's not awake, she's not asleep..." she said.

"It's all right dear, it'll be all right." His throat clutched and his heart felt dull. He dried his daughter's face and neck with a towel.

"You know this from your veterinary books?" asked Mary.

Gerald made no comment, and Mary left the room. Gerald's large frame weighed down one side of the bed as he searched the blankness of his daughter's open eyes.

"What were you doin' with that book?" He took her hand, hoping his voice would reach the place her mind had gone.

"Were you tryin' to read it yourself?" His eyes welled up. He felt helpless.

"Why were you sittin' by the window, Nessa? What did you see?"

Chapter Two

Townland of Disert, County Cork, May 1, 2009

The Wild Atlantic Way is both a philosophy of life and a two-lane road that twists along the rocky southern coast of Ireland, from Cork City south to Clonakilty, down the coast to Skibbereen, then north to Bantry and the Beara.

It's a road that demands respect, curling around outcrops of granite and flirting with thousand-foot drops to the foam and chop of the Irish Sea. I had to earn my way to the Beara.

Coming back from the States, I always forgot how bright the greens were, how damp the air; the *crump* of wave against cliff and the steady hiss of foam. The sights and sounds conjured the stories Da told at night, camping out at Mass Rock. He'd pace around the fire, playing all the parts, human and animal, complete with sound effects.

"Beware ye scabby tikes of the tall, thin and gho-o-o-o-stly sentinel who walk the coast at night. Their piercin' red eyes freeze the lonely traveler in 'is steps. With a grindin' shriek, the tall, red-eyed sentinel swivels the bones inside his skin with a sickening crunching sound, so 'is feet and knees point backward, and

his buttocks comes round the front. "Go to your home," warned the tall man, pointing his long finger, "Or I'll swivel your bones, too."

I felt a chill and turned up the heater. As the road turned northwest past Skibereen, I flipped the visor down against the lowering sun. Da followed his most terrifying tales with funny ones, especially when bedtime was near.

There once was a man who lost an eye in battle, and cried over the loss with his other eye. Fortunately, a gypsy healer was traveling by with a band of poets and musicians, and he agreed to replace the man's eye with an eye taken from a freshly dead cat. Although the man was grateful, there was a disadvantage to the arrangement. From then on, much to the man's embarrassment, his cat's eye would sleep durin' the day, takin' no notice of the goings on around, and at night it would open wide at every rustlin' reed and squeakin' mouse.

I smiled to myself and tapped a cigarette out of the pack on the passenger seat. ALS usually starts by killing the nerves in the hands and feet, leaving behind useless muscle. First, no more typing, then no more walking. Over two years it moves steadily inward until reaching the stomach, and the diaphragm muscles that open the lungs. With Da it was the opposite. The doctors couldn't say why the ALS went right for his diaphragm, but that's what it did. They called it "an unusual presentation." Suddenly he was stooped over.

Da had full use of his mind, and on Skype he seemed himself. I kept finding legitimate reasons to stay in the States, for not visiting just yet. Suddenly he was wearing a plastic mask for oxygen a few hours a day and taking morphine drops under his tongue. One day he couldn't take off the mask to talk, and I took the red-eye from Boston to Dublin, hopped to Cork City and rented a car. It had been four months since the diagnosis.

People of the Flow

The familiar outline of the harbor at Castletownbere came into view. I saw the bobbing, blue dot of my cousin Jeffrey's trawler. He hired me on for summers during high school. She was called *Manannan mac Lir,* after the Irish god of the sea. Jeff was still going out, now with his grown sons. It was good to see the boat out there.

Wired on coffee, regret, and adrenalin, I slowly rolled past the long row of narrow storefronts, each building painted a different color. Da said everyone did it for the tourists in the '60s, to sell postcards. I kept going past Da's pastel-orange storefront—*From Head to Toe*—where I started working at the tender age of six. Da had long ago cornered the market for accessories, from belts and ties to hats, scarves and gloves. Christmas and birthdays kept the family afloat.

Da was an even-tempered man, always charming with the ladies. It didn't matter to him what age, size or hair color, Da would look them in the eye and get his twinkle going. At the shop, he prided himself on never approaching a customer. As they came in and looked around, he would sit on his padded swiveling stool, talking to whomever had stopped by about the grievous weather, and what the fishermen were catching. Sooner or later, the customer would either join in the conversation or interrupt with a question. Either way, Da gave no indication that his life revolved around selling clothes. He was not a salesman. He was presiding. I asked him about it once: Why didn't he walk up to the customers and offer his assistance like they do in Cork City?

"That's backwards, son," he told me, swivelin' slowly on the padded stool to face me. "How do ya look bouncin' 'round the customer like a bunny rabbit? Like a man of authority? Far from it. I sit here on my stool like the wise man of the mountain, sought out for the knowledge I bring to the subject of quality accessory clothin,' which I happen t'have available. The whole idea is the customer comes to you. Don't chase your pennies and pounds, let them chase you."

I passed the end of downtown Castletownbere, beyond the last of the multi-colored downtown, heading west on R572. Butterflies were flipping around in my stomach. I pulled out another cigarette.

I didn't know what to expect when I told him after graduating from Cork City that I was buying a one-way ticket to Boston. I thought he might argue, question my reasoning, my haste, maybe get a little angry for once.

"The States, eh?"

"Yeah. There's no jobs here, Da—unemployment's almost twenty percent."

"You started talkin' 'bout America when you were just a boy. You wanted to know where the strangers came from every June."

I'm leavin', Da! Defend your hometown! Why can't I be happy here? Where am I goin' in such a rush?

"When I went to Cork City, y'always wanted the new American mags."

"Yeah."

"D'ya need money?"

"No, I'm good, Da."

I told my sister Fiona and my friends that I had to go. I wanted to see America, to have a chance. I only had to say it once. There was no argument, no questions, and no one wanted to hear it again. They were staying. I was spitting on the ground.

I slowed down and stopped for a dozen cows to pass. It was only a few miles west to where I grew up in the townland of Disert, a rocky pile at the edge of the Atlantic. Spanish sheep used to knock horns in the few grassy patches wide enough to be pastures.

Around that last corner, the white, clapboard house came into view, at the top of a sloping field, sitting at the base of a hill, out of the wind and rain. It was a sensible location in the shepherding days, but of little value in the modern market. Retirees prefer a view.

Two men were loading Da into a hearse when I pulled up. My stomach fell as I walked through the light rain, my sight a blur. A white sheet covered his body, and my sister Fiona told me I shouldn't look at him, but I had to. I had just run out of parents. The EMT pulled back the sheet.

Fio was right. Da looked like a puppet without strings. He wasn't there. That part of him that played the *bodhrán*, that laughed and smiled, that told stories and gunned the engine for his little boy, it was gone.

Chapter Three

Townland of Disert, County Cork, May 1899

After a short walk on a brisk spring day, cousin Abby was making tea in the kitchen.

Upstairs, Nessa was arranging herself in bed with a book when there was a rapping on the front door. Sitting bolt upright, she heard muffled voices and footfalls on the stairs. Da was on his veterinary rounds. Mum was visiting her sister in Allihies. Abby opened the bedroom door.

"Are we entertaining visitors today?" Abby asked, in a slightly silly voice.

"Of course," said Nessa.

A woman with long red hair and a kind face appeared behind Abby at the bedroom door. Next to her was a short, wiry man with a lopsided smile.

"Nessa," said the woman. "I am your Great Aunt Cara."

"Why do I not know you?"

"May I come in?"

"Yes."

Cara sat in a chair by Nessa's bed. The young man stayed by the door.

"In answer to your question, Nessa, you do not know me, nor I you, sadly, because of old family troubles, kept alive by some. I have no dark feelings. I only wish I was aware sooner that my little niece needed me. I am here for you, for your strength and health. This is my helper, Conleth."

The young man bowed his head. His *bodhrán* was decorated with rainbows and birds.

"How old are you now?" asked Aunt Cara.

"Ten."

"And why are you in bed on such a lovely day?"

"I have…spells. I take medicine. Bromide. It makes my stomach hurt."

"Mmm. Do the children tease you?"

Nessa was silent. Her eyes welled up. Cara took her hand. Her green eyes were kind. Nessa leaned over and whispered, "They called me a witch." Tears spilled onto her cheek.

Cara's eyes darkened for a moment, and she retrieved a handkerchief to pat away the tears. Then she spoke slowly and firmly. "Hear me, Nessa: They know not what they do. They know not what they say."

Nessa nodded.

"Sometimes my dear one, the gifts we receive are wrapped in pain. But you're a strong young girl, strong-minded. I feel it here." She put her hand to her heart. "You'll find the rest and peace you need inside your strength."

"How do you know I'm strong?"

Cara smiled and placed a hand on Nessa's heart. Cara whispered, "*Boom, ba-boom, boom ba-boom.*"

Conleth began to softly drum; "*boom ba-boom, boom ba-boom…*"

Cara sang in whispered words that Nessa didn't recognize. She closed her eyes, and the soft words danced in a circle, turning 'round so there was no beginning and no end. She was floating, peaceful. *Ba-boom, ba-boom.*

Suddenly there was nothing below her, and she was falling, reaching out. Her stomach lurched. There was nothing to hold, and she fell. In her ears was the sound of rushing water. She fell, turning and tumbling, wanting to scream as the rushing water grew louder.

The sound was coming from inside. The wind ripped at her arms and tore at her legs. She saw her body in pieces falling below her like parts of a doll, disappearing from sight. Nothing was left. Even her terror was gone.

Nessa heard her heart. *Boom, ba-boom.* Then her breath, in and out. Her thoughts felt light and loose. She heard the whipping of great wings, beating slow and steady. The wings were hers. The wind was hers.

Below her, treetops rushed by. A wide river snaked through the glowing, green countryside. She followed the river, coasting on the bright-blue wind. An island in the middle of the river stood above the currents, far below. Holding her wings still, she descended, gliding in a great spiral circle.

When she woke alone, the bottle of bromide was gone from the side table, replaced by a pot of steaming rose hip tea.

Chapter Four

Townland of Disert, County Cork, May 3, 2009

I woke up with the sun on my face, streaming through the window. I heard a scratching sound from above, then a thud. I slid up the window screen and poked out my head. Uncle Fran was straddling the peak of the roof, oiling the weather vane. I didn't want to startle him.

"Good morning," I said.

He turned and waved. "Good mornin' to ya!" He reached out and gave the swan a twirl. "The old girl's swingin' again!"

Fran wanted everything right for the wake. I kept trying to remember it was supposed to be a celebration. I went down to the kitchen, made a pot of tea, and went out to the porch for a smoke. A drop of water plopped into a bucket by the screen door every few seconds. Fran appeared in the doorway, looking up at the leak.

"That'll need fixin'," he said, taking a notepad from his back pocket and a short pencil from the wire binding. "I can fix a few little things before tomorrow, and the rest later."

In the kitchen, there were missing panes in the glass cupboards and a sizeable crack running through the plaster ceiling. Fran opened every window. Half of them slid down again.

"Sashes and weights are shot," he said, scribbling. On the second floor landing, the railing was wobbly, and the hall light was out.

"Gotta get in the attic," he muttered, handing me his flashlight. Standing three rungs up the stepladder, he popped a hatch in the ceiling and pulled himself up. I tossed him the flashlight and followed him up. I'd never been up there.

While Fran was checking the trusses, I picked my way toward a source of light, clearing cobwebs on the way. The board under my feet slipped and I turned my ankle.

"Shite!"

"Careful."

I put weight on the ankle. Only a twinge. I kept walking toward a small window at the front of the house. In front of the window was a child's rocking chair, and sitting on the chair was a square wooden box that looked old. A snake was sculpted on the top with some remnants of paint on it. There was a thin slit on top and a rusted lock on one side. I picked up the box. If there was something inside, it wasn't heavy. I shook it gently. Rustling. Papers maybe. I looked around for the key.

Knowing my family tree, I held out little hope for treasure. Still I searched various nooks and crannies, finding instead a book bound in green leather on a ledge. I blew dust off the cover. *Cormac's Glossary*. The title rang a far-off bell, from college probably. I put it on the rocking chair with the box.

After rubbing a clear spot on the grimy windowpane in front of the rocking chair, I could see the top of the lighthouse on Bere Island. I brought the box and the book over to Fran.

"I found an old box but no key." Fran showed his flashlight on the old lock.

"Looks a hundred years old, maybe more," he said. "I'd get a locksmith for it; be a shame to break it." We closed up the attic and I walked Fran to his truck.

"Ready for the wake?" asked Fran.

"Ready as can be."

"It's drink, dance and remember, Johnnie. Your Da wouldn't miss it."

Chapter Five

Miss Millington's Library, Castletownbere,
County Cork, June 1908

At seventeen, Nessa was tall for her age, with long orange hair, and when she rode into downtown Castletownbere on her Kerry Bog pony, the sight of her turned heads.

Nessa hitched her pony in front of the library, and walked up the familiar limestone steps, wondering how she was going to say goodbye to Miss Millington. Inside the bay windows, Nessa could see her reading to a dozen small children. Short and a little plump, Miss Millington's blonde hair was up in a bun. Nessa watched her slowly pace back and forth, gesturing theatrically with her free hand.

Over the front door was a sign with a single word artfully painted: *Leabharlann,* Gaelic for library. The sign was noticed when it first went up—Gaelic hadn't been taught in school for seventy-five years. For Nessa, it was a signpost to another world. Posted behind glass in the entryway was a paragraph written in impeccable calligraphy. Nessa stopped to read the words that first welcomed her to this place.

"We will show that Ireland is not the home of buffoonery and easy sentiment, as it has been represented, but the home of an ancient idealism. We are confident of the support of the Irish people, who are weary of misrepresentation, in carrying out a work that is outside all the political questions that divide us."

Written by the arts patron Lady Augusta Gregory, the poet W. B. Yeats, and the playwright Edward Martyn, the words were part of a letter that launched the Gaelic League thirteen years before. Now there were five hundred branches across Ireland.

Standing just outside the large reading room, Nessa watched Miss Millington telling *The Children of Lir* to a group of young children. Ever since she let it be known that the legendary *Children of Lir* were buried just outside the neighboring town of Allihies, the ancient tale had grown popular on the Beara.

King Lir of the Tuatha Dé Danann suffers the untimely death of his wife, whose sister becomes queen, wife, and step-mother to his four children, as was customary. But the king's grief for his wife and love for his four beautiful children left Queen Aoife alone, brooding, and jealous. Nessa stepped quietly into the reading room and sat in the back.

"One day the new queen led her four step-children to Lough Derravaragh to bathe and there transformed them into swans, decreed by spell to remain on the lough for three hundred years, and so they did," said Miss Millington, stopping to look at the children.

"But every night, when the swans sang, the otherworldly music was entrancing, and for three hundred years, people came to the shore in the evening and fell into a deep, healing sleep, from which they woke happy and refreshed. The very timelessness of the four swans' music made the years fly by."

Miss Millington paused.

"Finally, the spell lifted. Their wings and feathers fell away, and the swans became children again. Their beautiful music had kept them young, but everything in the kingdom had changed, and everyone was a stranger to them."

Miss Millington walked to the window.

"In their sadness, the children lost their spirit to sing and quickly withered into frailty and old age. They lived just long enough to tell their story and to express their wish to be buried together in a single grave, in Allihies, with their wings around them."

Nessa would miss her voice, her gestures, the soft light through stained glass, the smell of leather-bound books. When the class was dismissed, Nessa walked against a tide of children to greet Miss Millington. They sat together on a sofa.

"I remember that story well," said Nessa. "I hadn't the first idea what it meant."

"Better for the truth to unfold gently with children." Miss Millington took up her knitting.

"When the story says new queen turned her four step-children into swans, it means she drowned them in the lake."

"That's right." Her fingers moved neatly and exactly, adding a row of orange.

"The swans were their souls released from their bodies, singin' their true song on the journey to timeless Tír na nÓg."

"More or less."

Nessa had thought all morning about how to say goodbye to Miss Millington. When the moment came, her throat tightened.

"You've taken me to so many wonderful places in this room," said Nessa. "So many places..."

Miss Millington took Nessa's hand.

"When I first arrived here, this village was utterly strange to me," she said. "Now I'm dearly fond of it, most of the time. When you first arrive in Dublin, it'll be wonderful and ugly at once, but you'll not be alone. Agnes O'Farrelly is on the Board of Governors at Dublin University College now, and you'll be in the first class to include women, so she's excited to meet all of you."

"Thank you for everything you've done," said Nessa.

Miss Millington continued. "For thousands of years, the verses of the traveling bards called back the souls of ancient heroes in every townland." She finished another line of the sweater. "Now, without the bards to charm the heart of Ireland, the souls of Oengus and Aine, of Lugh and Danu, they only whisper in the wind." Miss Millington put down her knitting. "You, my dear, have the heart of a poetess. Your words can call them back."

Nessa smiled as her eyes welled up.

"Sometimes there are no words," Nessa whispered.

"You'll find them."

Chapter Six

Townland of Disert, County Cork, May 5, 2009

On a rainy Friday afternoon, Da's black coffin sat in front of the fireplace in the living room. Fio and I had split up duties preparing for the wake, avoiding the living room 'til now. With guests on the way, we took a minute to sit with Da.

"I was thinkin' about the games we played down by the cove," she said. "It was Da who started us on that pirate stuff. He said our people lit signal fires for the smugglers."

We heard tires crunch in the white-shell driveway.

"If I recall correctly, the great Murtogh McOwen Sullivan, man of the people, was famous for runnin' the coast durin' great storms to avoid the British revenue men, who were"—I coughed politely—"not willin' to risk their lives."

Fio smiled. I continued.

"Sullivan made a friend of the wailin' wind, his rudder partin' the ocean's white hair, off-loadin' untaxed rum and on-loadin' Beara wool against the mandate of Her Majesty the Queen, thereby gainin' the undyin' loyalty of the local farmers."

"You sound like Da."

"The key is to never finish a sentence."

We were quiet for a minute. Another car arrived.

"I believe our greatest neighborhood theater production involved you takin' Sullivan's hand in marriage."

"Any lass worth a shite would jump at the chance."

"It ended badly as I recall."

There were voices in the kitchen.

"Doomed from the start. The dastardly British revenue man Puxley shot us both in the back tryin' to flee our honeymoon cottage."

"You almost cracked your head tumblin' down the hill."

"Aye, the somersaults of death."

There were voices on the porch, then someone tuning a fiddle.

"I recall you oh so slowly dyin' by the water's edge, pledgin' eternal revenge on Puxley with your last breath."

"The limey bastard."

There were footsteps outside the sliding door.

"I'm sorry I wasn't there in time," I said. "I should have come weeks ago."

The punishing words had been running laps in my mind all morning: *No more chances, no more chats. Not now, not ever. You came back when you damn well felt like it.* My stomach rolled.

"No worries, John. It came faster than anyone expected. Da just ran out of fight."

Fio got up. "I'm gonna go manage. You stay."

I stared at the coffin, expecting something to happen. Listening to the light rain on the windows, I remembered the nicest thing Da ever said to me, on my rain-soaked graduation day at Cork City College. Emerging from the crowd with a big smile, dripping wet, he shook my hand, looking far more pleased than I felt.

"You're a block off the old chip, son, that's what you are, a block off the old chip."

I smiled at the coffin.

Through the sliding doors, there was murmuring and creaking floorboards. I wasn't keen on greeting a crowd of friends and relatives, most of whom I barely knew after twenty years in the States.

When Fio opened the doors, I never felt more like the son who left. After the ninth or tenth greeting, my fixed smile was failing and Uncle Fran saved me. At six-two, Da's younger brother was the tallest in the family. He put his arm around my shoulder and guided me to the porch. He lit a cigarette.

"Everyone liked your Da," he said. "Everyone. That's uncommon. Can't say as much for myself. So if I were sayin' the eulogy I'd say he's up in the clouds right now, ticklin' God's chin."

"I don't doubt it."

"You were lookin' a bit grim there, John. Supposed to be a celebration, y'know."

"I didn't get here quick enough to say goodbye to Da."

Fran put his arm around my shoulder again and looked me square in the eyes.

"Boy, you listen now. You don't put any weight on yourself that don't need to be there. Your Da loved you like no one else could. He wanted you to be happy and you went off to find it. Good for you. But don't you curse yourself. He wouldn't want it."

"I know he wouldn't—"

"There's an old tradition when something like that crawls up your arse," said Fran, with a look of firm intent. "Whiskey." He poured two shots and we drank them back. Fire in the belly. A fiddle started playing, feet began to shuffle, and smiles began to shine. Fio had invited some of Da's friends from MacCarthy's to play.

"Right," said Fran. "Lift them feet, boy!" And we did. When an unpleasant thought arrived, so did another shot of whiskey. I sang the songs I remembered, hummed the others, and played spoons on my knee. At one point a plump but pleasantly curvy middle-aged woman sat on my lap and gave me a boozy kiss. She went back to singing with the band, and a moment later Fiona sat down next to me.

"She's a fine Betty," I said.

Fio leaned over to whisper, "That's Alice Sullivan—she was Da's last fling. They'd been playin' together for years at MacCarthy's, before Ma passed."

"She's a looker," I hoisted my mug. "Good for Da."

"Not that I care whose box you're knockin' but you've got a eulogy to give in the mornin'. If you're gonna be in your cups, just take a tall glass of water every half-hour. You'll thank me."

Fio handed me a glass of water. The thought of being wooed by Da's ex was now having a sobering effect. I found Fran and thanked him for his kindness. After a final shot of whiskey, I wobbled up the stairs to my old room. The moon was just past full and the room was bright. I stepped on the sadness. Later on, it would be right where I left it.

Chapter Seven

12 Tara Street, Dublin, October 1909

Nessa felt at home amid the towering shelves and sliding
ladders of Harrington Booksellers. In the weeks before her first
classes, she had found it on Tara Street, between a clothing store
and a flat of apartments. The faint smell of musty leather reminded
her of Miss Millington's Library.

The young owner was usually reading behind the front
counter. Tall and thin, with an angular, clean-shaven face, Rigby
Harrington was matter-of-fact and distant at first. But when Nessa
returned a second, third, and fourth time, he saw that her interest in
foreign texts was genuine and well-informed and he softened.
They talked about his childhood as a diplomat's son in India, and
her fascination with faraway lands. They enthusiastically agreed
that the University's decision to accept women had been a long
time coming. When Nessa stopped by the fifth time, Rigby
welcomed her with a smile.

"It's good to see you, Ms. Ó Dálaigh," he said, tamping his
familiar Sherlock Holmes-style pipe. "How is the morning treating
you?"

"Couldn't be better Mr. Harrington, thank you for askin'. I'll
be needin' a copy of the *Rg Veda* please."

"Certainly." Nessa followed as Rigby navigated the narrow aisles, puffing his pipe. "Hinduism is my favorite religion," he said, stopping at a high bank of shelves lining the back of the store. "They always give you a second chance."

"How's that?"

Two rungs up the sliding ladder, Rigby looked back at Nessa.

"A Hindu can behave badly and go to a dark and horrible place after death, but there's always something virtuous one can do to get back in good graces, as it were. There's no such thing as a permanent sentence in the fires of hell, as some would have it."

Rigby retrieved the leather-bound book, climbed down the ladder and handed it to Nessa.

"I like the sound of that."

"Can I help you with anything else?"

"I hope so. One of my professors mentioned in passing a British author who found that Christian churches all open their doors to the east, facing the dawn. The trouble is, I can't recall the author's name. "

"Norman Lockyer. Right this way." Puffs of smoke trailed behind Rigby as he led Nessa down another aisle. "It's called *The Dawn of Astronomy,* " said Rigby, handing Nessa the book. "Mr. Lockyer is a celebrated physicist in London. It seems that while visiting the Vatican he learned of the tradition by which the doors of St. Peter's Basilica are thrown open at dawn on the vernal equinox so that the sun shines down the center aisle and directly onto the altar."

"How very pagan," said Nessa, following Rigby back to the front of the shop.

"Lockyer thought so too," said Rigby. "When he found that most every church in Europe is aligned to the rising sun, he set off to discover whether the ancient temples of Egypt and India were aligned the same way."

Rigby placed both books in a brown paper bag.

"What did he find?"

24

"I don't want to spoil the ending."

Nessa frowned.

"All right then, most of the ancient temples are oriented so the first rays of dawn on the winter solstice shine into the sanctum sanctorum." He lit the pipe until the smoke curled over his head. "There's an extraordinary example just up north in County Meath."

"A temple?"

"The prehistoric mound at Newgrange, by the River Boinne." Rigby scanned the price list.

"Brú na Bóinne?"

Rigby looked up. "You know it?"

"I do. Outside its entrance was said to stand a tree with silver branches, blooming flowers of purple crystal. The legends say Brú na Bóinne is a joyful, timeless place where no falsehood is spoken. George Russell wrote a poem about it: *A Dream of Aengus Oge.*" The little bell on the door jingled as two customers entered.

"I'm happy to say that George is a frequent customer," said Rigby. "We spent winter solstice morning last year at Brú na Bóinne waiting for the sun, but it was clouded over, so we're planning another attempt this year. I know George is a great fan of anyone with a fondness for the Brú, so you're certainly welcome to join us."

"Thank you, Rigby. I appreciate the invitation, and I'm pleased to accept. Do you think we might convince Mr. Russell to read a line or two on the occasion?"

"I can't imagine George turning down a chance to read his own work. He's been at the Abbey Theatre all week."

"Thank you again, Rigby."

She leaned over the counter and kissed him on the cheek.

"Your company is all the thanks I need," said Rigby, with a little bow. Nessa smiled back at him as she opened the door, which jingled as it closed. With new books in her possession, Nessa's step quickened. At the Abbey Theatre, she stopped to read a poster behind glass, written in exceptional calligraphy.

If you long for things artistic
If you revel in the nebulous and mystic,
If your hair's too long
And your tie's all wrong
And your speech is symbolistic;
If your tastes are democratic
And your mode of life's essentially erratic;
If you seek success
From no fixed address,
But you sleep in someone's attic,
Join the Arts Club,
Join the Arts Club.

Chapter Eight

Castletownbere, County Cork, October 2009

There were almost a hundred people at the Church of the Sacred Heart for Da's funeral. He would have been pleased.

Just a block away from his shop, the enormous, grey structure towered over downtown. Da's coffin sat in front of the altar. It didn't seem real. I didn't want to think about him lying inside that box.

There was an old, narrow, spiral staircase to the pulpit, where I found myself with my note cards. I'd written on top of the first card, "Remember to speak slowly." I started with Fran's line about how funny Da was, and that he was now in all likelihood ticklin' God's chin, which loosened up the quiet crowd. I talked about going with Da to the shop as a boy, learning about hard work, and knowing everyone in town by the end of grade school. I talked about the joy he found in later life, playing the *bodhrán* at MacCarthy's on Thursday nights. I said I'd be tryin' to bring Da's humor and kindness forward in my own life as best I could.

"I'll miss him every day," I said, and that's when my throat tightened up. I knew it would happen. There's nothing more silent than a church full of people waiting for the next sentence. Every sniff and whisper resounded in the vaulted space.

Fiona got up and approached the pulpit. As good a place as any for me to finish, I croaked "thank you," and focused on not tripping down the narrow spiral stairs and back to the pew. I could hear her turn the thin pages of the old Bible.

"I can't say that Da was a dedicated churchgoer," she said. "But when he and the boys got to playing at MacCarthy's, it lifted everyone's spirits. So the reading today is 2 Chronicles 5:13, recounting a truly miraculous musical moment at the dedication of King Solomon's Temple."

Fio paused briefly, as one does before a reading. It gives people a moment to cough or sneeze before the word of God is spoken. In a clear voice, she read the passage.

"It came even to pass, as the trumpeters and singers were as one, to make one sound to be heard in praising and thanking the Lord; they lifted up their voices with the trumpets and cymbals and instruments of music, and then the house was filled with a cloud, for the glory of the Lord had filled the house of God."

Father O'Meary took it from there. Dust to dust and all that rigmarole. In the front pew, Fio tugged my sleeve.

"Did you see? Did you see?"

"What? Did I see what?"

"Almost every last person in this church is wearin' somethin' they bought from Da's shop," she whispered. "I could see 'em all from up there. Mrs. O'Sullivan's green and blue scarf for sure, and Mr. O'Sullivan's brown cap that was on special last Christmas, and half-a-dozen others…" I looked around. With her eye for fashion, Fio would know better. She tugged at my arm. "They knew Da would be watchin' his own funeral," she whispered. "They sure as hell weren't gonna wear somethin' fancy from Cork."

I felt a chuckle coming on. "Who knows what favors a thankful soul might do in the Other World?" I whispered.

The chuckle gained a life of its own, which only tends to happen in the wrong circumstances. The idea that some goodly proportion of the town had worn somethin' from Da's shop for his funeral began to seem absurdly funny. I could see Fio's shoulders shaking.

Thankfully Father O'Meary finished quickly, and we managed to get away from the crowd. Behind the church, the giggles took hold. Fio was listing off the scarves and hats and who wore them when Father O'Meary appeared. We both stopped laughing. Father O'Meary smiled.

"I noticed it too," he said. "Never seen anythin' quite like it. Almost forgot what I was goin' to say, staring into the full range of inventory of your Da's shop."

I half succeeded at stopping another laugh—it came out as a snort.

"Thank you, Father," said Fiona. "You did a lovely job."

After the slow procession to the cemetery, we waited patiently as Da's casket dangled in mid-air for a moment. The groundskeeper banged on the winch, and it started again with a lurch. The priest said a few words I didn't really hear, and everyone walked slowly to their bicycles and cars.

"I'm sorry you missed talking to him one last time," said Fio.

"Me too." I kicked a stone. "How are Brian and the twins?"

"I'll find out soon enough. They're still too young for this sort of thing, and Brian was sweet to take them on, but now it's back to the house of squalor and poop." She smiled. "No place like home."

We arrived at her car.

"It's easy to imagine the levels to which those three might sink without you," I said. "I can see 'em now, bakin' a glue and crayon cake special just for you."

Fio smiled faintly, gave me a hug and got in her car. I gestured for her to roll down the window.

"Speakin' of property damage, Fran said he'll have an estimate on the old house soon, and then there's what to do with Da's shop. I'm thinkin' I'll come back soon…"

"You're always welcome, John, but there's no hurry. Aleksy's managing the shop nicely, and the house can wait." She rolled the window halfway up and stopped. "Don't forget to tell me about what's in the box."

"I will."

Fio waved and beeped, and briefly spun the tires. Just like Fio to kick up gravel in a graveyard.

Chapter Nine

Brú na Bóinne, County Meath, December 21, 1909

"And then there is the case of W.C. Borlase."

George Russell's low, barrel-chested voice sounded clearly in the pre-dawn cold. He stood on the Entrance Stone in front of the entrance to Brú na Bóinne. The stone was deeply carved with five interlocking spirals. Rigby and Nessa huddled in blankets as sparks flew from the campfire.

"Hailing from a wealthy family of respected archeologists, and a member of the British Parliament, Mr. Borlase was a cultivated man whose appetite for fine food, drink, and voluptuous women devoured his assets and sent him into debt. Finally, he was publicly humiliated in two languages after withholdin' the usual financial support for his Brazilian mistress."

Nessa giggled. Rigby smiled and relit his pipe. George continued.

"So. Mr. Borlase is drummed out of Parliament, shunned by his own family, and chased by heckling creditors until he flees to Ireland and becomes a tax collector. In his spare time he becomes enamored with this very place, and writes a book called *The Dolmens of Ireland* in 1897, in which he disputed the notion that it was a passage tomb, and concluded instead that Brú na Bóinne was a temple where ancient Celts would come to fast for days in the pitch black of the chamber, to experience visions."

George retrieved a bottle from his rucksack. He poured a jigger into Nessa and Rigby's outstretched tin cups, and fixed a cup for himself.

"A touch of whiskey as the hour draws near," boomed George, holding up his tin cup. "To W. C. Borlase, whose book changed the direction of my life."

"Cheers!"

The faint sound of swans calling drifted from across the river.

"I was here last spring when the swans flew north for the summer," said George. "It was extraordinary. The entire group was callin' out and flappin' their wings—" He paused.

"And?" asked Nessa.

"It's hard to describe—I'm not sure it's really a dance, but I suppose that's close enough, like a grand ball, hundreds of swans flappin' their wings and jumpin' up and down, callin' faster and faster, and finally they lift off, one wedge after another, flyin' off to the north, to Iceland, or so I'm told."

George looked at his watch, drank the dregs from his cup and picked up the lantern.

"Come!"

Rigby and Nessa followed George as he climbed over loose granite and tree roots to an open area just above the entrance to the passage. George kneeled and set down the lantern.

"If you two come without me someday, this is the trick."

George slowly pulled a rectangular block of white quartz from an inset of granite until it lay at his feet. Rigby took hold of a second block and dragged it from the setting. What remained was a thin rectangular opening above the entrance.

"Like opening a window," said Nessa.

"Exactly," said George. "Now the final piece."

They made their way back down the mound, to the main entrance, where George hung a heavy tarp over the opening to the passage.

"Perfect!" said George. "Open the window and close the door." He pointed to a thin slab of granite at their feet. "The builders used that slab to seal the opening, but they had more people. The tarp is good enough. Come on."

Turning aside the tarp, they entered the passage one by one.

The roof of the corridor was only about six feet high. George hunched over slightly as he played his flashlight on the massive granite boulders to either side. About thirty feet in, he stopped.

"Here in the middle, the passage moves slightly to the east."

He shined the flashlight up and down the stone corridor. "You see the turn? It narrows down the beam of light reachin' the chamber. Undoubtedly purposeful."

They walked another thirty feet and emerged into the round central chamber, which opened upwards to a dome more than twenty feet high.

"Incredible," whispered Nessa.

"It's a corbelled dome," said Rigby. "No mortar."

George set down the flashlight pointing up, and the small room brightened. The walls were made from stacks of flat granite slabs, each one reaching out a bit further towards the center of the room, forming a dome. Most of the stone surfaces in the chamber were decorated with etched spirals, waves and triangles.

At the back of the chamber, opposite the passage, Nessa ran her fingers inside the smooth bowl of an ancient granite basin. On the wall above and behind the granite basin, she saw a water stain. The face of the stone was damp to the touch.

"There really is a winter-running spring here," she said. "They built the mound around it."

Nessa traced one of the spirals with her finger, out to the edge and back to the center. Words came to her mind, as if spoken. *That which turns...*

"The Tuatha Dé Danann were shape-shifting water spirits," boomed George, his low voice echoing slightly in the rock chamber. "It is said they arrived on the coast in a fog, and crossed the coastal headlands, gliding over lakes and floating through forests until finally stopping on this very hill, where they discovered a winter-running spring."

"The People of the Flow," said Nessa.

"Exactly so!" boomed George, through his bushy red beard. "Complete mastery of the waters, in every form. Traveling on the waves, shrouded by mist, playing the harp inside a crystal palace at the bottom of a lake, or setting anchor on a cold spring by a turn in the river."

"How old is this place?" asked Nessa.

"Timeless," said George. "No one knows. The latest guess is 2,000 B.C."

Rigby tapped his watch. "We've just enough time for a few words, George."

They stood by the basin in the back recess of the chamber. George cleared his throat.

"And even as he spoke a light began to glow and to pervade the cave and to obliterate the stone walls and the antique hieroglyphs engraved thereon, and to melt the earthen floor into itself like a fiery sun suddenly uprisen within the world, and there was everywhere a wandering ecstasy of sound: Light and sound were one; light had a voice, and the music hung glittering in the air." The words echoed away. The darkness softened.

"There's sunlight in the corridor," whispered Rigby.

They all looked down the stone-lined corridor.

"It's coming."

Approaching slowly, the shifting beams of light seemed to flow forward down the passage, more here and less there, stealthy and bright. The central chamber slowly

filled with an ambient glow. Words came to Nessa without thought: *They played*

music when the light came down the passage.

A narrow beam of sunlight passed into the chamber, lighting

the basin. Nessa unscrewed her canteen and poured water into the smooth bowl. The thin beam grew wider and sparkled on the water in the basin for almost a minute. Slowly moving away and across the chamber, the beam lit up the spirals, waves and triangles etched in the stones, as if unveiling an ancient story.

The beam began to shrink, and Nessa reached out her hands, turning them in the golden light. They watched in silence as the beam steadily backed away toward the passage and finally disappeared.

Nessa followed the sun out of the chamber and down the passage. The two men went after her, out the entrance and up to the top of the mound. Nessa squinted east at the rising sun, then turned west. In the brightening morning, she saw two smaller mounds to the west, each about sixty feet across. Breasts above the womb. She pointed.

"George, are those what I take them to be?"

"Yes indeed. The word Brú meant many things: house, mansion, womb."

"The womb is quickened by the dawning sun on the winter solstice," said Nessa.

"One might say," said George. "A divine birth of spring to come."

"Hard to deny the layout," said Rigby, puffing on his pipe. "Any bloke would tell you the landscape here looks like a large woman lying down."

"A goddess," said Nessa, sitting and leaning back on a boulder. "Reclining."

She arched her eyebrows at Rigby.

"Waiting for the sun."

Chapter Ten

12 Tara Street, Dublin, October 2009

Behind the counter, the white-haired man sat with his back to me. Under a bright light, his white-gloved hands manipulated the delicate mechanisms of an old clock.

"Good afternoon," I said.

He turned quickly. I expected an older fellow, the last of the artisan clockmakers. He was maybe twenty-five, with hair dyed white, and he wore a small gold ring in his nose.

"Yeah, mate?"

"I figured this was the place to come for fine motor skills. I'd like to have an old box opened without breaking the lock."

"Let's have it then."

I took the old box from my backpack. The young man's eyes opened wide.

"Why that's class, that is." He looked it over until he came to the cobra. "Jayzuz. Fine work."

He put the box under the bright light and took out a tiny brush. An old man came through the door behind the counter. Same eyes, but his white hair was earned.

"What have you got there, boy?"

The young man bristled. "Not a boy," he said under his breath, carefully applying oil to the lock mechanism with the little brush.

"Name's Paddy," the old man said. We shook hands.

"I'm John. I brought this box to be opened."

The old man looked over the young man's shoulders.

"Lovely. Do you know what's inside?"

"No."

"Brilliant. Could be anything. Could be treasure."

I smiled faintly. Paddy took a closer look at the box.

"Looks to be a cash box, late nineteenth century," he said. "That's a fine serpent. How'd you come across it?"

"I found it in the house where I grew up, on the Beara in County Cork."

"Mmmm," said the old man. "I'd be a buyer at 175 euro. Just the box—not what's inside."

The offer surprised me. "No thanks."

"Family heirloom," said the old man. "I understand. What do you think Martin? Are we ready?"

"Oil's set."

He fiddled for a bit, turning a pick in the lock. After a couple of tries, we all heard a distinct click. Martin smiled and presented me the box.

"Nice job," I said, opening the lid.

Inside was a clipping of orange hair on top of a thick stack of yellowed envelopes wrapped in twine. Peering into the box, the old man smiled and raised his eyebrows.

"Hmm," I said.

"No telling what form a treasure will take," said the old man.

Chapter Eleven

Aer Lingus Flight #1505, Dublin to Boston, April 13/14, 2009

The overnight flight to Boston was filling up, and so far the seat next to me was empty. I kept an eye on the people coming down the aisle until two were left; a large man and someone obscured behind him. The large man passed by to reveal a short, older woman with bifocals. I helped put her bag in the overhead bin, and we sat down. She was tiny.

"Mirella," she said, offering her hand. I shook it. She wore her gray hair in a ponytail and wasn't hiding her wrinkles. I guessed she was about seventy.

"John."

"I bet you were happy when you saw me comin'," she said, settling in her seat.

"I would say that yes, your diminutive stature is pleasin' to me in this particular circumstance."

"Do you like to talk or not to talk?" she asked.

"Some of both."

She smiled. "You're quick enough."

"Thanks."

Upon the beverage cart's arrival, we had determined that she was a genetics professor at Trinity with two daughters, two grandchildren, an aching back and a paper to give at a conference in Boston in two days.

By the time the cabin lights were dimmed, we had further determined that my Da had just passed, I'd never been married, that I'd better get working on my "commitment issues," and lastly, the passion that drove me to become a small town newspaper editor was fading under the new corporate owner. After toasting to our meeting with nips of whiskey, Mirella put on a sleeping mask and we both eventually nodded off.

The cabin was dark when I awoke. Unfastening my seatbelt, I retrieved the old metal box from the overhead bin. The lid squeaked, but no one stirred. Under the orange lock of hair was a folded piece of paper. I adjusted the overhead light and unfolded the single piece of thick bond paper. Inside was a black-and-white photo of a tall, thin man with his arm around the shoulders of a woman almost as tall, with long, flowing hair. They were standing next to a large oval stone, with five big spirals etched in it. Above and behind the stone was the dark opening to a passage, topped with a flat slab.

Across the top of the bond paper was old-fashioned script lettering.

"Marriage License, Docket of Dublin County."

It was signed by Rigby Harrington and Nessa (Ó Dálaigh) Harrington, married on May 15, 1911. Nessa was Da's grandmother. Under the marriage certificate was a stack of yellowed envelopes tied in a century-old twine knot. I loosened the stack and pulled on the strings until I squeezed the top one out. The envelope was addressed to Major Rigby Harrington, British Army Service Corps, No. 7 Labour Company, El Kantara, Egypt. The return address was Nessa Harrington, Harrington Booksellers, 14 Tara Street, Dublin. The top of the envelope had been slit cleanly open. I slipped out the letter. The ink had faded, but not badly. The penmanship was graceful.

My only Rigby,   December 16, 1915

One of the singular benefits of working in your bookshop is
engaging in a passing conversation on the meaning of spirals in
Neolithic art, as the crowds bustle by on a busy afternoon. So it
was when Francis stopped in today to purchase Mary Czaplicka's
Shamanism in Siberia, and he asked for a glass of water. When I
provided one, he dropped in a handful of sand and pebbles,
inspiring a case of curiosity in a gentleman browsing nearby. We
both watched as Francis took out a pencil and stirred the water in
the glass.

"What happens when we make a spiral in the water?" he
asked.

Neither I nor the nearby gentleman had an answer. Francis
continued to stir.

"What happens to the sand?"

"It rises," I said.

"Exactly." He stopped stirring. "The Entrance Stone at Brú na
Bóinne is covered in spirals. It means: This is a place for the spirit
to rise." He paid for his book, and off he went.

Little Daniel is doing very well helping me run the bookshop.
He loves for me to hide in the back while he sits behind the front
counter and surprises the customers, who are surprised to find a
four-year-old boy in charge of the cash box. It gives him a thrill.

Your Uncle Edward arrived yesterday, and I've been soaking
in his bookish wisdom every minute. I see a family resemblance in
the cheek and jawline, but he's smaller overall. He was pleased to
find the shop is paying its bills on time and generating a modest
profit.

Edward says the newspapers are not reporting yet the scale of
the casualties in France, and that hundreds of thousands are dead
or injured. Daniel is curious about the war, and asked me so

sweetly the other day, "Why do they fight?" I found myself
without words. What should I tell him? What should I tell myself?

I never thought I would be deeply thankful for your poor
eyesight. I imagine you in a quiet office typing dispatches, far
away from the carnage., so I am thankful. Your absence is like a
ghost in the house. I often sense that you're upstairs or in the
garden. I miss you most after Daniel is asleep. In the light of day,
walking to the bookshop, I worry about Daniel's future in this city,
with so many poor souls living in such desperate circumstances. In
the streets, the odor of sewage can be overpowering. I don't wish
Daniel to feel as powerless as I do in the face of such misery.

I saw a priest on the street last night who looked very much
like Father Kerry from Castletownbere. I remembered sitting in the
pews as he barked about the devil abiding in our flesh, thrusting
the donation-basket on its long stick under our noses, one by one,
promising salvation in exchange for silver. It's a terrible injury to
young minds to be shamed for sins they haven't committed, to
begin the needless cycle of guilt and deliverance. I can't watch it
happen to Daniel.

There's a grade school not far from the bookshop that was
founded by the Gaelic League in 1898; at least during school hours
Daniel would be spared the nonsense of the priests. I'll be taking
him to visit next week. I plan to volunteer there and hope for a
permanent position once you've returned to me and the bookshop.

I was thrilled when Mr. Hyde's analysis of our ancient
manuscript finally arrived last week. With just burnt fragments, he
found it difficult to be certain of anything, but he believes it was
made in the eighth or ninth century. I barely slept over the
weekend. I believe there is enough in the pieces of artwork to
make out more than one swan, and a woman's mouth blowing into
what appears to be a fluted antler. It reminded me of Diodorus
Siculus writing of the mythical Hibernia, on a far north island,
where the sun god Apollo enjoyed a choral service each spring at

an ancient round temple where human singers performed
harmoniously with a chorus of swans.

And so because I need little excuse to flee the present world,
I've spent every free moment revisiting the swan legends from
Ireland to Siberia, and piecing together a story. It seems I have
little choice in the matter, as the words keep running across the
page, line after line, racing to some unknown end. Douglas
believes as I do, that old stories are like old rugs—they must be
taken out every so often and slapped about, so they might regain
their color and depth. If we have only fragments, it's best to fill the
gaps between with imagination than leave them sorrowfully blank.

There is certainly no better time to resurrect the Tuatha Dé
Danann than today, when much of Ireland seems to have forgotten
them. While the meaning of the name is generally taken to be,
'Tribe of (the goddess) Danu,' I have come to favor a different
meaning, one that seems more fitting to me:"People of the Flow."
After consulting your handy tome on etymology, and asking
Edward's advice, I now prefer the underlying meaning of Danu as
descriptive of a river, as in the Danube, which some speculate the
Celts used to reach Old Europe from the Black Sea. Danu meant
river, just as Boinne means river. It also means, not surprisingly,
"flow." Thus, instead of Tribe, of Danu, one might say instead,
"People of the Flow." Edward noted that it's consistent with the
Dananns' arrival in Ireland on either a wave or a cloud, and their
subsequent travel inland by mist. The name also satisfies the Celtic
fondness for double- and triple meanings, in that People of the
Flow also describes the Danann talent for the finest musicianship
and verse.

I hope you enjoy my reconstructed tale of Danu, which begins
in Iceland, circa 2,200 B.C. May it take you away from the day
you expected.

People of the Flow

In the cold air of late October, whooper swans flew from all over Iceland to a long, shallow cove on the southeastern coast. They honked through the night and in foggy weather so the rest could find their way, and as each family arrived, they called and danced in greeting. The air was filled with conversation as they foraged for food, fattening up for the long trip over the ocean.

On a clear night, after a week of grazing, a full moon rose from the sea. As faint stars arrived in the darkening sky, the Song of Flying began with soft trilling sounds, slowly growing in volume and pace. As the voices of a hundred swans called and bugled, they flapped and hopped and danced on the beach, and in the shallow waters.

From the shore, a human voice joined in suddenly, clear and beautiful. Danu stood on the beach in a dress of white feathers. A yellow stripe was painted from the corner of her eyes to her mouth, like the whooper. Her strong voice kept pace, and harmonized with the whoopers' song. One of the swans approached her, bobbing and squeaking. Danu knelt and opened her long, slender fingers. The swan turned its head in Danu's hand, trilling and squeaking, before rejoining the flock.

A dozen women emerged from the trees with antler-flutes and bell-branches., gathering in a circle on the beach, dancing counterclockwise. When they lifted their arms, they seemed to grow wings.

Joined by a new chorus of voices, a thrill went through the flock of whooper swans. Some of the more brave-hearted swans swam to shore and joined their two-legged cousins , bugling and hopping on the sand.

When the pace reached a point when wings and feet and limbs could move no faster, the whoopers ran over the waters with wings flapping, slowly lifting off into the sky. In the bright moonlight, they called out at every wing-beat: *Whoop-ah, whoop-ah, whoop-ah*, as they flew to their winter grounds.

As one wedge after the next rose into the night, the women on the beach danced until the cove grew still. Filled with dreams of flying, they slept on the shore.

*   *   *

My dearest Rigby…when I lie in sleeplessness I sometimes feel the strong warmth of your body like a gift in the night, your eyes, your face, your arms and scent…a kiss, then many. I love you Rigby, through the darkest hours of the night.

 Yours always,
 Nessa

I heard a faint sigh. Turning my head, Mirella met my eyes with a grin. "I was reading over your shoulder," she whispered. "The penmanship is so lovely and the writing…it's so romantic. No one writes like that anymore. Who is Nessa?"

I told her about finding the letters and retrieved the box from my knapsack under the seat. She held the box in her wiry hands, and looked closer. She traced the etching of the cobra with her fingers.

"How beautiful," she whispered, opening the lid, and taking out the lock of orange hair. She held it up to my reddish-blonde hair.

"Now that's genetics," she whispered, returning Nessa's hair to the box. "Shall we read another?"

She smiled.

"I can never sleep on these flights anyway," I said, adjusting the overhead light. The next letter was addressed to Nessa Harrington, Harrington Booksellers, 14 Tara Street, Dublin. It was written six weeks after the first.

44

People of the Flow

My Lovely Nessa,   January 2, 1916

I've taken up the habit of climbing to the Crow's Nest just before dawn while most of the crew still sleep. It allows me time to smoke, read your letters and think without interruption.

It would be impossible for you to write too often. I cherish the picture of Daniel behind the counter, greeting my loyal customers. I'm certain the Gaelic League will do a fine job with his education, never mind the pleasant instruction of your bedtime stories.

Did you know the English celebrate a day in spring when they officially and quite literally count all the swans on the Thames? It's very important. The monarch is present when the total number is announced. Unfortunately I have no idea what it means, and neither does anyone else.

With regard to the war, I'm equally pleased with my poor eyesight, and have no wish to take up arms. A recent skirmish in the biblical setting of the Sinai reflects how difficult to grasp this war can be: A British commander in charge of Indian forces turned back an assault from Turkish troops led by a German general.

I was pleased to hear Uncle Edward had arrived. I was nine years old when he took me to Sir John Soane's Museum in London. I recall staring in disbelief at the large, coiled serpent carved onto the top of Seti I's sarcophagus. That a serpent was sculpted on the coffin seemed strange; up to that point I knew the snake only as a symbol of temptation and evil. As we moved through the exhibits, Edward explained that pre-historic peoples used the qualities of animals as part of a symbolic language. That day I think my fate to dwell on all things old and dusty was sealed. I followed Uncle Edward into antiquarian books rather than following father into the diplomatic service.

It appears I will have a welcome break from army meals tomorrow. I've become acquainted with an Egyptian labor broker named Gamal, who's invited me for a meal at his neighborhood cafe in old Cairo after the market closes. He is short and round with a well-kept moustache, born in Thebes and well-educated with a young family. His grandfather was a Habib, a kind of Muslim cleric.

BONG! The intercom crackled and the cabin lights came up. "We'll be starting complimentary breakfast service…" We looked at each other and kept reading.

Regarding the meaning of "Tuatha Dé Danann," I believe "people of the flow" is both a fair and compelling interpretation. You might consult George. I'm sure he'll agree. I thoroughly enjoyed the beginning of your Icelandic saga—the notion that people could once communicate with animals is universal, and you have managed to render it believable. If anyone can breathe life into the old legends, it is you. Your passion for the nature religions is one of many, many reasons why I love you. I see you sitting by Daniel's bed, your shawl about your shoulders, reading him fantastical tales.

I never knew to hope that I would someday meet a woman with such gifts of mind and spirit. Looking at the photograph of us together at Brú na Bóinne keeps me purposeful. I know I will return because it cannot be otherwise. I love you dearly.

Yours,
Rigby

I glanced at Mirella, to see if she'd finished.

"Oh, I just love them!" she said, her white ponytail bouncing. "He's very logical, but sweet."

"I didn't know much about them 'til now." I showed her the old photograph with the large stone covered with deeply etched spirals.

"Oh, they're a lovely couple. That stone is familiar…" She adjusted her biofocals and looked closer. "I think that's the Entrance Stone at Newgrange. It's a Neolithic mound up in County Meath. Very famous."

The tiny airplane on the video screen was closing in on Boston, and the flight attendants were offering coffee, tea or juice, and mini-muffins.

"When you're done reading them, you ought to send a copy to the library in her home town. Was it Castletownbere?" said Mirella, stirring in the sugar. "I'm sure they'd love to have letters written during the Celtic Revival. It's the hundred-year anniversary." I agreed.

When the plane landed, the familiar beep and boop of typing on iPhones mingled with a dozen one-way conversations and the rustling of bags. I helped Mirella with her bag and walked with her to the taxi stand outside. She pressed a card into my hand.

"Let me know how it comes out."

She waved out the window of the taxi, and I waved back. I made a note to scan the letters at the office and headed off to long-term parking.

Chapter Twelve

The Cape Paper, Orleans, Massachusetts, April 18, 2009

There's something ghostly about an empty newsroom. Gone is the constant chatter and tapping of keys, the joking and debates. At ten-thirty on a Tuesday night, *The Cape Paper* was ready for bed except for a late story from the Wellfleet Town Meeting.

I went through my In box while waiting for Melissa to get back. As an unrepentant dinosaur, I preferred to edit on hard copy, which meant I was one of the few newspaper editors still working with In and Out boxes. My young staff thought it was cute.

I also clung to the notion of sitting down while working, which was rapidly becoming old-fashioned. Most of the young staff were now standing up at their new high "desks" ($600 a pop) to avoid back problems and, I can only guess, the insidious pooling of blood in the buttocks.

I heard the outside door open and footsteps on the stairs. At six feet, Melissa was a force to be reckoned with on the volleyball court, and on the beat.

"Whaddya' got?"

"What's that old round thing on your wrist?" she asked, sitting down.

"A watch."

"Why not use your phone?"

"My phone is for talking, my watch is for telling time."

"Life's passing you by, John."

"From where I sit, that's fine with me."

My reporters were all in their twenties, all looking for the story that would seal their reputation as not-to-be-fucked-with. No inspiring speeches were required to wind them up. It made my job easier.

Like any good reporter, Melissa wanted nothing more than to see her name above a story that everyone was talking about. There's something about having your work published 12,000 times that puts a skip in your step.

"Whaddya got?"

"They spent half-an-hour on buying a used snow plow for the dump truck and five minutes on the three million dollar school addition."

"Let me guess." I lit a cigarette. "Some guy's cousin could get a cheaper snowplow from some guy he knows. And those old plows are built to last, not like the new ones."

"More or less." As usual, Melissa's copy was clean, with one or two exceptions. I typed out the headline: *Thumbs up for old snowplow, new school*

"Nice," she said. "I got something else."

"What?"

"Can't tell ya."

"Not the funky news dance."

"Gotta show ya."

Melissa held her hands high above her head, and turned slowly around, pumping her arms like a runner in slow motion, and swaying back and forth.

"Give," I said.

She sat down and flipped open her notebook.

"There was some really fun stuff towards the end…what I like to call Town Meeting Theater."

My ears perked up.

"It started with Chuck MacGibbon reading from *The Lorax*, by Dr. Seuss as a commentary on Hanson's new development next to the Audubon Refuge. Then—"

"Perfect. Love it. Write it up."

Twenty minutes later, Melissa delivered a story ready-made for the warm embrace of the printing press. I pulled up the front page to find a spot for it. That's when I saw a box in the corner titled *Citizen of the Week*, with a picture of an old woman in her garden.

"What the feck is this?"

Melissa looked over my shoulder.

"Oh yeah, right—corporate got the results of that phone poll while you were gone. Sixty-five percent found the newspaper to be more negative than positive or something like that, so they decided to fix it with a Citizen of the Week. Check your email."

I scrolled through my email for a message from corporate, and there it was: "Citizen of the Week: Creating a positive reader experience."

I hit delete.

"Should I laugh or cry?" I asked.

Melissa shrugged. "Suit yourself."

All I knew was Melissa's story would fit perfectly in that little box on the front page. It was the easiest call of the day. I deleted the Citizen of the Week, laid in the new headline over Melissa's story. It fit perfectly.

Lorax Sighting in Wellfleet

By Melissa Long

Performance art or political theater?

A fictional creature and a bag of marbles were both enlisted last night in the ongoing battle against John Hanson's development abutting the Audubon Society.

"The Lorax is a short brown creature with a bushy yellow mustache," said Chuck MacGibbon, reading to a captive audience at last night's Wellfleet Town Meeting. "He speaks for the trees and tries to stop the Once-lers from building a factory."

The crowd murmured, someone giggled. MacGibbon continued in a deep and sonorous tone, without cracking a smile.

"The Once-lers are crazy with greed and use Super-Ax-Hackers to cut down Truffula Trees, which results in the loss of the habitat for Brown Bar-ba-loots. That's all I have to say."

The crowd applauded, some laughed. On the way back to his seat, MacGibbon stopped to present a copy of *The Lorax* to John Hanson, the developer in question.

But the performance art wasn't quite over. Kelly Young gave Hanson a bag of marbles. She returned to the microphone to report that she presented the marbles to Hanson "because he seems to have lost his." The moderator pounded his gavel.

"Let's have no personal remarks."

As for Hanson, he smiled and nodded, but declined to offer a response. After the meeting, he painted a silver lining. "Dr. Seuss and a bag of marbles," he said. "Now I don't have to shop for my five-year-old's birthday."

*   *   *

"I love it," I said, bumping fists with Melissa.

"They're not gonna like that you killed the Citizen of the Week," she said.

"It deserved to die."

"So the Lorax might live!" Melissa shouldered her knapsack and headed for the stairs.

"Thanks," I said.

"My pleasure."

I looked over the front page once more and sent it off to the press. I lived for the perfect headline. Just as great sculpture is said to live within the wood or the stone, waiting to be released, the perfect headline emerges from the fragrance of events.

I leaned back in my chair, the flip-phone chimed. It was a text from Uncle Fran with the estimate for repairing the house. "Expert says foundation slipping. High water table. Might not be worth fix. Sorry."

Even if we did well enough selling Da's shop instead of taking rent, we weren't going to make the number Fran texted.

Before shutting off the lights, I retrieved the Citizen of the Week email from the trash and typed a response to corporate: "Negativity is the hallmark of a free press. By definition, we shine a spotlight on greedy/irresponsible/idiotic scumbags that plague the decent people of this world. How else do we build a more perfect union?"

I smiled and hit "send." I wasn't going to be the saluting sap who put *The Cape Paper* on the happy road to positivity. It was bad enough that AllTown Media required my reporters to be on Twitter—the unsigned road to hell, paved with one hundred and forty characters.

It was a perfect moment to enjoy the cliché of pouring two ounces of whiskey from the bottle of Tullamore Dew I kept for just such momentary flights of grandeur. The smooth fire warmed my belly.

It had been a year since Malcolm Smollett signed the weekly newspaper he founded in 1957 over to his son Fred, who promptly sold it to AllTown and bought a house on a lake in Vermont. Malcolm had vision and integrity to spare, but at the end, it was dementia that got him. It was hard to watch him go quietly those last few months, wandering into that good night.

Meanwhile, AllTown was buying a hundred little weeklies all over southeastern Massachusetts, selling their downtown offices, moving the stunned staff to an office park and laying off photographers, all to make that twenty percent profit they promised the shareholders.

The Cape Paper had avoided the worst of it. It already turned a well-above-average profit, boosted by the summer of course, so the folks at corporate left well enough alone. Our leash was loose, for now. I poured a second shot of Tullamore Dew, and drank it down. Feeling less wired from deadline and more comfortable in my chair, I took out the old metal box. The scales of the serpent on top were still faintly colored in yellow and green.

I opened the top, and flipped through the stack of envelopes, counting seven letters. Beneath them was a little book with a clasp, like a diary. I would read the letters one at a time, and then the diary. No rush. I took out the third envelope, adjusted the overhead light and settled back in my chair.

My sweet Rigby,   January 21, 1916

Most everyone who comes to the shop talks of the horrific casualties in France and elsewhere. Yet one of the joys of managing the bookshop is that every day brings something fresh and unexpected. George came by after another trip to Brú na Bóinne, where he watched two whooper swans going through an extensive greeting, calling out back and forth, quite distinctly, as if singing a duet. It reminded me of something I'd heard in Professor O'Farrelly's class—that it was the habit of the Irish king every night in his bedchamber to sing half-a-quatrain, and the queen would sing the other half.

I find myself thinking more often of New York City, where John Mitchel is mayor—an Irish-Catholic nationalist. It's a city where Daniel could be proud to be Irish. At Columbia Franz Boas is establishing the first proper School of Anthropology, beyond the reach of the Catholic Church.

If I'm not daydreaming of America, I'm visiting the past. The day we first visited Brú na Bóinne has become the most beautiful prism of memory—the glowing beam entering the dark chamber and the sparkling play of light in the water of the ancient basin. The memory inspires me. Here is the latest of Danu …

*   *   *

Just inland from the whoopers' cove, under a natural rock overhang leading to a series of caves, Danu and the feathered women began a school of music and language, teaching new sounds and rhythms of speech. Each student made a cloak of feathers and journeyed to the shallow highland lakes to observe the swans through the summer, to learn the rhythm and melody of their calling and conversation.

Over the winter, in the echoing caves, Danu delivered a melodious flow of words and phrases, turning like a river, breaking over rocks and swirling in eddies. The mission of the school was to craft a language that could stir the deepest wells of feeling.

Every year, new boys and girls came from distant villages to learn the language. At night they lit fires and held tournaments of dueling poets who parried back and forth, inventing stories through the night. In late October, the students' families came for a tournament of storytelling, and to sing the Song of Flying with the swans.

The Icelanders admired the swan's elegant beauty, its stately poise and musical voice. They admired the whooper's power and ferocity in their own defense. And so the mystery deepened…where did they fly every fall? Where did they spend the long months of winter? What lay beyond the horizon of the southeastern sea? As the December nights grew longer, it was Danu's story of the whooper's mysterious winter home that moved the people to gather closely around.

Danu told of the swans flying south in the fall, calling out past the horizon to a bright river of stars, steaming in the cold darkness. Through the winter, Danu pointed out the starry cross-shape of the swan in flight, carrying souls to the northern celestial pole, the timeless pivot point of space, around which every star turns.

In late December, Danu's people watched hot-white stars shoot out from the celestial pole, flying toward the misting Milky Way. In spring, they saw the star-bird descend to the horizon, and the swans returned, carrying souls made young for spring.

In time, the Icelanders planned a journey, eager to prove the stories true. They would follow the swans southeast to their winter home, sailing over unknown seas.

*   *   *

I'll fix a hot brandy and milk now, and try to sleep. There's no moon tonight, and Cygnus is flying bright. Perhaps you're looking at the same stars, at the same time.

Yours always,
Nessa

Chapter Thirteen

AllTown Media Corporate HQ, Dedham, Mass., April 19, 2009

The next morning I had an email directly from Asa Martin, the HR director for AllTown. That was a first. I called him.

"John, how are you?"

"Fine, good, well as can be expected, thanks."

"Listen, you've gotta come see HQ. We've been here a year now, and you've managed to avoid it. I think it was the flu, a sprained ankle, and a sick cat, if memory serves."

"I don't own a cat."

"I know it's off-Cape, but it's only a ninety-minute drive. Come on down and let me show you around. There's good people here. Plus we have some new management protocols I need to tell you about."

"That doesn't sound good."

"All good, all good."

I played the Super Hits of the '70s all the way to Dedham— my antidote for simmering annoyance. If *Le Freak* and *The Night Chicago Died* couldn't improve my mood, nothing would. Just off Route 495 was a campus of square buildings and parking lots. I pulled into a space near the AllTown Media building and took the elevator to the fourth floor. Asa had a big corner office.

"Welcome to HQ!" Asa said, coming around his desk to shake my hand. "Have a seat. I was sorry to hear about your father. Completely understandable if you want some time off. Of course, the private sector has yet to adopt the kind of sophistication I'd like to see with regard to the grieving process, but you can use whatever sick days you have. I looked it up—you've got almost a month. It seems you only get sick when there's an event here at HQ."

He laughed heartily and sat down.

"Right."

"I'm only kidding, of course, you're one of our best people, John, really, one of our best people."

Asa rocked his chair back and forth. He was one of those guys with more energy than he could handle. HR people often had a bubbly personality.

"So." He rubbed his hands together. "New management protocol. Just came down. Voluntary retirement payouts. Bring up the next generation, that kind of thing."

"Voluntary?"

"Yes sir, voluntary at this time, yes, sir."

"At this time?"

"Never know what's coming down the bend right? Never know. Internet's been killing business. We're in it, of course, building that web presence, starting to make a little something on the bottom line. We're good, good."

"I wasn't thinking of retiring yet Asa, I'm only forty-four."

"Let's see." He looked at his computer. "Eighteen years in. Payout's eighteen months of salary, plus benefits. Totally voluntary. Hey! Let me show you around."

Asa led me to a short hallway, which opened into an endless sea of cubicles. I walked down one of the aisles and saw a pennant sticking up in the air. I walked closer. It read, *The Taunton Gazette.*

I kept walking, and soon there was another pennant, reading, *The Attleboro Sun-Times.* The air suddenly seemed thin. I took a deep breath and kept walking. The next pennant read *The Somerset Times Weekly.* I could see two more pennants in the distance.

A young guy with a short ponytail was typing away in a nearby cubicle.

"Where was the paper located before moving here?" I asked.

"I don't know, I wasn't here, but I think it was in downtown Somerset somewhere."

"Thanks."

"Sure."

I walked back toward the elevator, past *The Taunton Gazette.* Taunton was twenty miles away. All of these local newspapers had given up their post on Main Street for a cubicle by the highway just to rake in some short-term capital. I felt vaguely nauseous. Asa was talking to a woman a few cubicles over. He intercepted me at the elevators.

"Hey, did you know this building used to be a parking garage?" he said.

"Really."

The world was closing in.

"Hey John, what about that Citizen of the Week? I've heard it hasn't appeared yet in the *Paper.* Everyone's very excited about it around here."

The elevator arrived and I stepped inside. Almost out.

"We're still working on the protocol for the background check," I said.

Asa put his arm between the elevator doors.

"What background check?"

"We wouldn't want the Citizen of the Week to have a criminal record, like indecent exposure in a playground or something."

Asa looked blank.

"That would be bad," I said.

Asa looked puzzled, then worried. The doors closed. Going down, I slumped against the wall and closed my eyes, trying to shake the image of a six-story parking garage full of weekly newspapers, each flying their little pennants. Back on the highway, my head was crowded with violent thoughts and snippets of depressing poetry, a byproduct of my degree in English Lit.

"So this is how the world ends…pinned and wriggling in a cubicle…" I noticed I was doing eighty-two in a sixty, and eased off the gas pedal.

I said a silent prayer for all the cub reporters who'd never get to sit at Malcolm's knee and learn what a gutsy newspaper is all about. I was done.

Chapter Fourteen

Bohernabreena, County Dublin, May 1910

Rigby held the reins and Nessa sat beside him as the wooden wheels of the swaying cart rolled over a hard dirt track, behind a pair of brown ponies. It was a brisk May morning with a troop of white clouds floating slowly by.

"How many interviews have you conducted?" asked Nessa.

"Thirty-five."

"Still no title?"

"I was considering *Supernatural Stories of the British Isles*."

"Perhaps the perfect title will come to you once you've finished."

"*The Faerie Faith in Celtic Countries*?"

"Better."

Crossing an old stone bridge, Nessa exclaimed at a field of white lilies growing along the marshy edge of the river ahead, and Rigby steered off the track. She took his hand stepping out of the cart, and they walked along the riverbank.

"The early Irish saints waded into rivers to pray, for hours," said Nessa. "It's said if you listen long and closely enough to the wind and rush of water that voices come whisperin'."

"What might they say?"

"They might say that beauty is all around us, but we must choose to see it." For a long moment they watched the river rush past.

"I remember Hindu women wading into the Ganges, wearing bright silk bandhani saris embedded with tiny mirrors. The saris floated out behind them in the water, and the little mirrors sparkled in the sun."

"What I would have given as a young girl to be whisked away to India. I'd like to visit one day. I believe I'd enjoy riding an elephant."

"I believe all of India would enjoy seeing you ride an elephant." The clouds were growing heavier. "We should get on." Back at the cart, Rigby put up the old leather top before getting underway again.

"How did you find this man, the seer?" asked Nessa.

"He came by the bookshop the very first day I was open, asking about the most recent Eastern texts translated to English, and he's been a loyal customer all along. It was just a few months ago when I told him of my research into the fairy faith, and he promptly invited me for a conversation on the subject, on the condition that his name is withheld."

"Why?"

"He's a vice president at the Bank of Ireland."

The cart emerged from a copse of trees and into a flowery meadow, at the head of which was a large stone cottage with white smoke coming from its ancient granite chimney. Rigby pulled up in front and paused, waiting for signs of life.

A tall, middle-aged man came onto the front porch, neatly attired with a white linen shirt and grey wool pants.

He waved.

"Come in."

The smell of smoldering peat and tobacco welcomed them inside the dim cottage. They made introductions and settled at the kitchen table with a steaming pot of tea, a warm loaf of country bread, butter and honey.

"I hope you enjoy nettle tea," said the seer, inviting Rigby and Nessa to sit at the kitchen table.

"Thank you, I do," said Nessa.

Rigby opened his notebook. "Nessa will be graduated from University College Dublin next month. She'll keep your confidence."

"As long as my name is withheld. My colleagues wouldn't take kindly to my prattling on about faeries."

Taking a seat in a well-used chair by a small window, he began whittling on a piece of wood.

"Can you tell me about the Sidhe?" asked Rigby, pronouncing it *shee*.

The seer focused on his carving as he spoke. "The Sidhe exist in a timeless place of the ever-young, in Tír na nÓg, where one sees nothing save beautiful forms and hears nothing but harmonies."

"Is there a location for Tír na nÓg? Is it a physical place?"

The seer sharpened his pen-knife on a worn stone.

"I believe it's not so much a place as a condition of the natural world, a kind of latent potential in the air and water that's stronger in some places than others. At certain times, in these certain places, the veil comes away from the other world and a gateway opens between the two."

Nessa watched a robin land on the windowsill.

"What have you seen?" asked Rigby.

"Glimpses only, enough to break my heart. The first time I saw the Sidhe with great vividness I was lying on a hillside alone by Brú na Bóinne: I was listening to what seemed like the sound of bells, an ever-changing silvery sound. Then the space before me grew luminous, and I saw a dazzle of light that came from the head of a tall figure with a body that was...opalescent. I could see through it, but I could see it was there."

"Semi-transparent?" asked Rigby.

"Yes, opalescent."

The wood block was taking on a rounded shape in the seer's hands. Nessa put down her teacup. Her cheeks were slightly flushed. The seer kept whittling.

"Can you describe the tall figure?" asked Rigby.

The seer looked up. "Words are inadequate."

He started whittling again.

"You said you saw them vividly," said Nessa.

"Words are still inadequate, but I can tell you what I saw." He stopped whittling, and looked out a little four-pane window. "Throughout its opalescent body ran veins of electric fire. Around its head was waving, luminous hair blown all about like living strands of gold. Light streamed from its head in every direction."

"What effect did it have on you?" asked Nessa.

The seer looked up at Nessa. "The effect left on me was one of extraordinary lightness, joyousness…ecstasy."

He retrieved a tin of snuff from his shirt pocket, inhaled from the back of his hand and returned to whittling.

"I would easily have stayed with them if I could."

"Who do you think they are?" asked Rigby. "I believe the Sidhe correspond to the Tuatha Dé Danann, the first recorded inhabitants of Ireland. They were men and women once, unusually tall, but men and women just the same. Now they are not. They are Sidhe. I must assume they learned how to pass through some kind of window or gateway, to become something else. It's said the gateway is inside Brú na Bóinne, which is why I chose that place to lie on the turf. To listen."

"What is their purpose?" asked Nessa.

"In our mortal state we have no way of knowing. It is a far higher state of being they inhabit, a kind of constant renewal. It's said they play music from the other world that heals the sick."

Nessa squeezed Rigby's hand. The seer returned to whittling. The round shape was becoming more oval.

"Do you know of others with similar experience?" asked Nessa.

"An old schoolmaster in the West of Ireland described them to me from his own visions as very tall, beautiful people, and he used some Gaelic words, which I took as meaning that they were shining with every color. More tea?"

"Thank you," said Nessa.

The seer refilled their cups and returned to whittling.

"Brú na Bóinne was built where the salmon spawn in fall and where the swans have their winter grounds. The old books say prize dogs were brought there to breed. It may well be that on the morning of the winter solstice, the mound was a place of conception for the royal families."

Nessa looked at Rigby, who lifted an eyebrow.

"That's a curious thought," he said.

"Not really," said the seer. "Have you forgotten the Dindshenchas?" He got up and pulled a book from his bookcase. "From the tenth century." He flipped through the book. "It talks about the Dagda having sexual relations in the Brú na Bóinne.Ah!"

He found the page he was looking for, and started reading.

"Behold the bed of the Dagda, he paid noble court after the chase, to a fair woman free from age and sorrow. Behold the two paps of the king's consort, beyond the mound of the fairy mansion."

"The mound of the fairy mansion is Brú na Bóinne," said Rigby.

"And the two paps are the smaller mounds to the west," said Nessa.

"Yes, and yes," said the seer.

"The winter solstice represents rebirth," said Rigby.

"Reincarnation is more accurate, I'd say," said the seer. "From June 21 to December 20, the sun slides further south on the horizon each morning until its warmth is barely felt. During the night of December 20th—the longest of the year—the sun is infused with enough power not only to stop its southern trajectory, but to start moving north again along the horizon. It represents, I believe, the power to return from death, and start life again, the power of reincarnation."

"The Tuatha Dé Danann were known as masters of rebirth, they were able to guide their souls into the next life of their choosing," said Rigby.

"True enough," said the seer. "We all know the story of the Danann's surrender to the Milesians, and their agreement to disappear under the ground, and under the waters. This was a way of saying they were all killed in the battle, or killed themselves, and their spirits went under the ground, and under the waters. But as masters of rebirth, where do you suppose they chose to reincarnate?"

"In the bellies of the Milesian queens and princesses," said Nessa. "To grow up in the castles of their conquerors."

"Slick as a whistle," said the seer. He put down his whittling and looked out the window. "If I was young and in love and starting a family, I'd take my bride to Brú na Bóinne on a winter solstice morning. You might attract the soul of Aengus."

He smiled at Nessa, and handed her the carving. It was a swan.

"Thank you. It's beautiful."

"Please, call me Francis. You'll be seein' me at the bookshop at one time or another."

Francis led them out to the porch, where they said their goodbyes. Back in Rigby's cart, Nessa turned the wooden swan in her hand.

"Rigby, do we have any plans for the winter solstice?"

"I can think of nothing else."

Nessa leaned into Rigby's shoulder as they rattled down the hard dirt track to Dublin.

Chapter Fifteen

Wellfleet, Massachusetts, April 16, 2009

I woke up early, took a shower and made chai and toast. Fio had texted, asking me to call, so I woke up the Skype machine and typed her number. The back of a child's head appeared on the screen.

"Fio?"

"Hold on." She rearranged Liam on her lap.

"Is he four now?"

"Just turned."

"Ahhh look at him, he's a dote. How's the shop?"

"Aleksy's doin' a fine job, makin' rent every month, and everyone's stayin' on."

"Is he still talkin' 'bout buyin' the shop?"

"He's not mentioned it lately."

Liam grabbed Fio's nose. She brushed his hand away.

"How're ya keepin'?" she asked.

"Well enough." I told her about the letters, and the tiny old woman on the plane. I promised to scan the letters at the office, and send out PDFs. As I talked, Liam was trying to make his escape down Fio's leg.

"Brilliant," she said, pulling Liam back on her lap.

I told her about the sliding foundation at Da's house in Disert, and Fran's estimate to repair it.

"No surprise there—that old place 'as been goin' sideways from the start. Only a matter of time."

Liam settled down. Fio patted his back.

"You're takin' it well."

"Ah John, me childless brother—I've learned to take things well."

"Fio, what do you know about Da's grandparents? That wood box Fran and I found had a stack of old letters in it. Rigby was serving in Cairo during World War I, while Nessa was running his bookshop in Dublin."

"I don't remember the name Rigby. Wasn't there a Nessa married to Harold?"

Liam was pulling on Fio's sweater.

"Shush Liam, just another minute."

"The marriage license says Rigby, and she writes to him as Rigby."

"I thought his name was Harold. Da didn't talk much about them."

"I don't remember one way or another, but I'll look into it."

"Have fun. I'll be swabbin' vomit from the dishware."

She pointed the laptop's camera at the dishwasher. The dishes and silverware were covered in brownish goop.

"Yech."

"Liam's gettin' over the flu. Seems the dishwasher was just the right height for explosive barf. Gotta go."

"Bye, Fio, bye, Liam!"

Tapping away on the keyboard, I soon learned that many of Britain's military records had burned during the bombing of London in World War II. Still, I paid the necessary fee to view what remained, and typed in the search window, Major Rigby Harrington, No. 7 Labour Company, El Kantara, Egypt.

His military record popped up. It showed he enlisted in Dublin on June 12, 1915, with the British Military Service Corps. There was a note in a box at the bottom of the page, in tightly scrawled script. I zoomed in and made out the words: "Deserted, June 17, 1916." The next line read, "Warrant issued June 26, 1916." That was the end of the record. Rigby fled the war. The penalty for desertion in WWI was death. Why did he do it? Where did he go?

He might have changed his name to Harold and disappeared into the townlands of the Beara with all the Irish Harringtons. I searched the parish death records. There was no Harold Harrington of the right age, and the records were pretty thorough. They'd been on-line for years, largely to encourage the seventy million Irish out there in the world to search for their ancestors and come back "home" for a visit. I made a cup of chai, got out the old tin box, and turned the lock of orange hair in my fingers. Family colors. The next letter was from Rigby.

My Lovely Nessa,   February 12, 1916

It's just after dawn, a beautiful morning in the Crow's Nest. I continue to enjoy your story immensely. It was clever to choose Danu as the main character; she's known to be the great mother of the Tuatha Dé Danann, yet she's rarely mentioned in the legends. That some early proto-Celtic people developed a more sophisticated and lyrical language by listening to swans is not unreasonable, considering the adoration of the whooper swan among the northern peoples. What is a bag-pipe after all, but a swan with three necks? If ancient Icelanders followed the swans to Ireland, it would not be the first or last time that divine motives inspired the migration of a people. I'd much rather Irish children read your story than the latest Shilling Shocker and Penny Dreadful...

I would be happy to venture to the New World with you and Daniel. It would be a grand adventure. New York is a good market for antiquarian books, and with Uncle Edward's shop in London, we could form a trans-Atlantic partnership, and outflank the competition. I would be happy to leave the Old World behind. It is showing an ugly side that stains the rest.

Meanwhile, it brings me no great joy to report my promotion to captain of the No. 7 Labour Company. One benefit is I'm in charge of reading/censoring the men's letters this week,, so you may find a bit more freedom in my expression, at least for the time being. (I hate the duty. It makes me feel like a Peeping Tom.) The promotion came about in the following manner:

During the past year, our Egyptian and Mesopotamian Expeditionary Forces competed for labor and supplies, in the Egyptian markets, causing prices to rise. In response, the Home Office formed The Resource Board (to which I am now assigned), which will purchase all supplies and hire all laborers for every branch of the service. Having enjoyed the benefits of playing one branch against another, the Egyptians are unhappy about the formation of the Resource Board. Relations were already strained by a story going around about a British officer flogging an Egyptian laborer on the Isle of Mudros. The uneasiness of our alliance is no great surprise. We've withheld the tools and equipment that might build an industrial sector here, just as we've done in India, to protect our manufacturing monopoly back home. We've taken great tracts of land in both countries.

I mentioned meeting Gamal in my last letter, and can now regale you with the most fascinating two days I've spent in some time. After a day of haggling over the price and abilities of available labor for the Sinai railroad, Gamal and I walked together to his neighborhood, beginning with the bathhouse, one of the oldest in the city. On the first floor they tend vats of boiling water stirred with herbs and oils, and the steam rises through vents to the second floor where it warms a series of stone masseurs' tables.

Upstairs, steam rises from small holes in the stone slabs. The room is thus filled with steam and the scent of spices, and one lies down to receive a rubbing of oil and herbs.

Afterward we each indulged in a snifter of absinthe and cigars at a nearby café, and I told him of my visit to Soane's Museum as a child in London, and that my encounter with the serpent on the sarcophagus of Seti I was partly responsible for my enduring fascination with ancient cultures. I expressed my disappointment in the British government for not requiring the return of Seti I's sarcophagus and other treasures. Gamal was pleased with my sentiment and told me of his grandfather, who took him on trips to the old ruins up and down the Nile as a boy. Gamal said he brought his sons on such adventures when they were young. I told him of you and Daniel running the bookshop in Dublin, and our visits to Brú na Bóinne, and Dowth.

There is a certain excitability in the effects of absinthe and soon we decided on a brisk walk through a maze of outdoor markets and alleyways until we rounded a corner to behold the Sphinx and the Great Pyramids. The night was cloudless, and the stars were bright, let free to shine by the dim, crescent moon.

The war is a terrible beast, but it has brought me to a place without equal. I was immediately struck by the immensity of the structures. They are in total command of the landscape. Gamal said the original appearance of the pyramids was even more striking, that they were originally covered with polished, white limestone and a massive quartz capstone. He reminded me that the rising sun hits the highest point in the landscape first and descends, so the sun would have lit up the sparkling capstone first, as Gamal said, "like a fire lit from heaven."

Staring at the Great Pyramid, it struck me as identical to the three-sided facet atop a column of crystal, with the rest of the stone sunk deep into the sand, static and immoveable, but somehow charged or "connected." (It may have been the absinthe.) In contrast, the Sphinx seemed poised to leap. Despite the general perception that the Great Pyramid is a tomb, Gamal said none of the excavations have turned up a sarcophagus or any indication that someone is buried inside. He said the ancient Egyptian Sed festival was celebrated next to a pyramid every three years. The festival began with the pharaoh lighting a flame, and its purpose was renewal and reinvigoration.

As we walked back, I told Gamal of our first excursion to Brú na Bóinne—the spirals etched in the Entrance Stone, the dawning sun creeping along the passageway on the winter solstice and lighting upon the ancient basin. Right off, Gamal invited me to the Temple at Karnak, where he said he would show me similar practices. I asked if he knew the meaning of the word Karnak, and was disappointed to hear the old Egyptian meaning is lost. In Arabic, it means "window," which is, after all, an opening where the sun enters.

I arranged a Sunday furlough the following week and we enjoyed the journey down the Nile, arriving at the ruins of the temple in mid-afternoon. Words still escape me. I cannot possibly convey the immensity and mass of the carved pillars, nor the sheer size of the sprawling site. Lockyer believes the first temple was erected there, circa 3,700 B.C.

We walked a thousand feet along an arrow-straight stone path between rows of rams with spiral horns, standing figures with arms crossed, past harpists and tambourine players. Each section of the path grew increasingly narrow until we stood outside the inner sanctum.

Gamal said that on the winter solstice, the dawning sun follows the narrowing path we had just walked, until it arrives at the sanctum where it is further framed by a small square window. Inside was a block of stone and a sloping floor with a drain still visible on the lower end, meaning they must have used water in the ritual, perhaps not unlike the basin at Brú na Bóinne. Gamal's grandfather told him that in the inner sanctum, there was once a statue, inset with gems, which sparkled in the sunlight. I had only one wish at that moment, and it was that you were with me. The majesty of the ruined temple, the size and elegance of the attending statues—the hair stood up on my arms.

Meanwhile, I believe there is a book of photographs from Egypt in the shop—aisle three, I believe, near the back. Perhaps you could show it to Daniel and tell him his father is living near there for a time, and that I'll tell him all sorts of stories when I get home. Whenever I imagine you and Daniel, it lifts my spirits. You both shine on me from afar. I love you dearly and miss my little son. Hold his hand for me.

Yours always,
Rigby

Chapter Sixteen

Brú na Bóinne, County Meath, December 21, 1911

Sitting against the granite wall of the central chamber at Newgrange, Rigby filled his tobacco pipe, tamped it down, and lit it with a wooden match. There was an orange fragrance to the smoke, which curled away into the darkness. Nessa reached over and took the pipe. She puffed twice and handed it back.

"Thank you, my dear."

In the predawn dark, a lantern flickered at their feet.

"Bru is one of those words that has the same meaning on many levels," said Rigby, puffing away. "In Old Irish, it means womb, and in Gaelic it means house, mansion or fortress."

Nessa leaned into his shoulder and put her arm in his.

"The Bru is where Diarmait and Grainne slept as runaway lovers," she said. "Where the Dagda and Boann conceived Oengus...Oengus who became a swan to be with his true love."

Rigby squeezed her hand.

"When they found this place in 1699, there were half a dozen smooth round stones in the basin of the east recess, right there."

"Like eggs," said Nessa.

Rigby puffed the pipe. The smoke coiled away in the dark.

"I've always admired the Celtic celebration of women," he said. "I've always thought of them as elegant, beautiful, somewhat mystifying creatures, certainly to be celebrated. And investigated."

Nessa took the pipe from his mouth, and took another puff.

"Soon enough," she said. She got up and walked to the basin at the back of the chamber. She traced her finger in a triple-spiral etched in the granite at the back of the chamber, across from the entrance to the corridor. "The goddess reclines…"

"What's that?"

"If I were a naked goddess, I would like to recline with my breasts to the sky, like the Paps of Anu…"

"Hmm," said Rigby, putting one hand around Nessa's waist and the other on her shoulder.

They waltzed slowly around the chamber in the flickering dark. On their fourth turn the chamber began to glow with ambient light. They stopped dancing and went to the chamber entrance, where they watched as the sun brightened the corridor. As a wide beam of sunlight approached, they returned to the back of the chamber and undressed. Rigby folded his pants and laid them on the floor next to his shirt and sweater. Nessa threw her clothes in a pile, and soon they lay in each other's arms on a bed of sheepskin.

A beam of sunlight entered the chamber. Nessa watched the beam approach over the hard-dirt floor of the chamber. *They shaped the light. They narrowed the beam.* She closed her eyes and felt the warmth of the sun on her feet and shins, moving slowly, steadily. She felt soft heat on her knees, then her thighs.

Nessa made a little sound of pleasure, and slowly opened her legs. The rounded beam of light was six inches across. *They narrowed the light.* She felt the warmth of the sunlight between her open legs, unlike anything…Nessa reached for Rigby, and in timeless rhythm they moved with each other in the first light of the Celtic year. The beam of light sparkled on the basin of water behind them.

People of the Flow

In the northern sky, high above the great mound, the Ursid meteor shower sent white-hot rocks streaking out from the celestial pole, about five to ten per hour, flying into the steaming Milky Way.

Chapter Seventeen

Newcomb Hollow Beach, Wellfleet, April 19, 2009

The sound of ocean waves on the beach, one after another, resets the mind. Sometimes, when the wind blows hard enough, a mist whips back from the crest, and the sun hangs a rainbow in the spray.

"Hey, John."

I looked up.

A nineteen-year-old college student named Charles T. Conrad lay down his bike and sat next to me on the beach.

"Holy...what's up, big fella?" I said. "It's good to see you."

"I saw your car—figured you were down here."

I'd known T since he was in second grade, when I volunteered for a lunchtime reading program, mostly to impress my girlfriend at the time. I patted the sand next to me. He sat down.

"How's B.U.?"

"It's good. One of the teachers was a jerk, but the others were OK."

"Jerks are the worst. They spoil everything."

T smiled. "I did OK."

"What's on the menu for summer?"

"Same as last year, putting up tents for special events…"

T's father left when he was four, and T had been disrupting his second grade class, so he was chosen for the one-on-one reading program. They told me he was two grades ahead in math.

The first day, he chose one of the Harry Potter books for me to read while he ate his cafeteria fish sticks, pudding and carrots. He seemed like a good kid. Very polite. Then again, I was twice his size.

Eventually, we lost the Harry Potter book but found a nerf football and went out in the snow, where I played quarterback to his diving-to-make-the-incredible-catch wide receiver in a big snow bank behind the school.

Two weeks after school ended in the spring, his mother Shelly called to say T was wondering where I was. Listening to her voice on the phone, it dawned on me that T probably wasn't fond of men disappearing on him.

Most every Sunday I stopped by at noon, went inside to say hi to his mother Shelley, and together we made sure T had whatever he needed like mittens or a hat. There was a lot of biking on the rail trail with backpack lunches, there was bowling, mini-golf, and soft-serve ice cream. There was backgammon or Stratego over lunch at Jo Mama's, and whale-watching. There was sitting on the lawn at Cape League baseball games, somewhere near the ice cream truck. And, of course, there was ping pong: The Rite of Passage.

"How about we head back to the A-Frame, get somethin' to eat," I said.

"All right."

We headed up the mile and a half trail through what T used to call the "spooky woods." The scrub pines were short and knotty, with limbs twisting in eccentric directions from the constant wind.

"How was Ireland?"

"I dunno, I'm still sort of in shock from everything, and then add jet lag on top, and it's like everything's moving in slow motion. Then today, AllTown Media offers me a buy-out."

"What does that mean?"

We paused to watch half a dozen wild turkeys crossing the trail up ahead, pecking and bobbing their heads. They got moving into the forest when we started walking.

"It means they pay me and keep me on the health plan for a year, but I don't go to work. Instead, they pay someone who's a lot younger a lot less money, and it pays off for them down the road. Plus I think I'm beginning to be a pain in their ass."

As we approached the A-Frame, the last two turkeys disappeared into the trees.

"What are you gonna do?"

I opened the door for him and he went into the living room.

"I think take the money and run. If I stay, I'll get used to it. I'll get comfortable."

"What's wrong with that?"

"Nothing." I sat in my lazy boy in my living room. T sat on the couch. "The problem is, I just got a look at the future of small town newspapers in eastern Massachusetts, and it's a former parking garage off 495 in Dedham, or, as I am beginning to suspect, the portal to the gaping maw of hell itself. I don't think I can get comfortable with that. Would you like a beverage?"

"I'm OK."

I got up and put two mugs of apple cider in the microwave.

When we first started hanging out, I expected a seven-year-old boy would ask one question after another, which I was dutifully prepared to answer, passing on the bounty of my knowledge to the younger generation. As it happened, T wasn't much for asking questions at first. So I asked him questions. Turns out, he wasn't much for talking, either.

Not being a big fan of extended silence among fellows, and recognizing that I had a captive audience who looked up to me, literally, I proceeded to tell one tale after another about my career as a knight of the keyboard, and out there in the field, covering fires and deadly car crashes, murders and other awful things. Many of these recounted tales reflected well on me. Sometimes I tested whether T could sniff out exaggeration. He could, with a sideways look.

I soon noticed that he watched what I did and listened to what I said, *all the time.* Suddenly, I was more careful about holding doors for strangers, and struggled not to indulge in rude language.

Back at the A-Frame, I started some toast to go with the cider.

"Blueberry jam ok?"

"Not the weird kind."

"There's no such thing as weird blueberry jam."

According to a Big Buddy Program brochure I'd picked up twelve years earlier, the mentoring philosophy was simple: Don't try to be a parent. Discipline is not your job. Just have a good time. Be the one person in his life who doesn't require anything. So I didn't tut-tut him, and I wasn't nosy. I was actually his big buddy. As I brought the cider and toast into the living room, I had a feeling something was up with T, but he probably wasn't going to tell me what it was.

"Hey," I said, "I was gonna watch Kung Fu, waddya think?"

"What's that?

I was used to the ignorance of the young. It no longer bothered me that my cultural signposts were fading away, ultimately to be lost forever.

"Kung Fu was a great TV show back in the early '70s about a wandering monk who kicked ass in slow motion."

"I never heard of monks kicking ass."

"Only when it's truly necessary," I said. "Hold on a sec, it's better with chocolate pretzels." I gathered the goodies and retrieved the VHS tape. "Did you know that in the span of my lifetime, the VCR has gone from the newest, coolest thing in the world to useless junk?"

"Yeah."

"And just when they invent the biggest most high definition TVs ever made, like 75 inches wide, suddenly all you kids want to watch stuff on a screen the size of my hand. Why is that?"

"I don't know."

When I was T's age, I was a lot more talkative. In fact, I was more than happy to explain things I knew nothing about, so I took it as a sign of maturity that T frequently answered my questions with "I don't know."

I clicked on the TV and queued the aging VCR.

"Aah, yes. There he is. Kwai Chang Caine, walking the western desert under the beating sun."

On the couch, T watched closely. I provided running commentary from the lazy boy.

"And here's the gang of scumbag thugs…and there's the ugly insult about yella half-breed Chinamen. I really *hate* those guys."

One of the thugs ran at Caine with a piece of wood raised in his hand.

"And there he goes—right through the window!"

I rewound a few seconds.

"Check out the slo-mo. This is the first TV series that used slo-mo. Check out the shards of glass falling all over the scumbag!"

I took a bite of the chocolate pretzel.

"Woohoo!"

T was smiling. Success! I had resurrected another lost gem of the 1970s for the next generation. I paused the show to explain the flashbacks to Caine's childhood in the Shaolin Temple.

"These are the best parts," I said, restarting the show. "Young Caine is meditating in the temple but suddenly becomes disturbed and cries out. Master Kan approaches."

Caine: "I heard the sounds master. I felt my whole being diffused like a cloud. Then rain fell from the sky, through me. I was part of everything, but I was myself."

Master Kan: "You have experienced oneness."

Caine: "Yes master, but in this great joy, I felt as if I was dying; that is what frightened me."

Master Kan: "What you felt in the silence was real. Something in you is dying...it is called ignorance."

T watched closely. I tried to remember whether Caine was a Taoist or a Buddhist. As Caine set off for the next town and the credits rolled, I asked T what he thought.

"It was cool. He was good. I liked it."

Effusive praise. We walked out on the front deck and sat on the steps.

"T, you know, I've never been nosy about your personal life, right?"

"That's true."

"Now that you're not a kid, that's all gonna change. What's bothering you?"

"I met a girl, and we went out most of the year, and she just dumped me."

There it was. Puppy love. The worst kind of hurt.

"Shit, I'm sorry. That's a punch in the gut. What's her name?"

"Alice."

It didn't require telepathic powers to tell he didn't want to talk about it.

"Lucy and I are quits too."

"When? I liked her."

"Couple of months ago. I liked her too. But she seemed more interested in making sure she got married before turning forty than anything else. I got the feeling I was a prop in a play that I wasn't sure I wanted to be in."

"How many is that now?"

"How many what?"

"Girlfriends since I've known you."

"When I was your age, I figured I'd be a dad by now. I s'pose I better figure it out or it'll never happen. Women can be a real puzzle. Or maybe I'm one of those guys who likes the euphoric beginning more than what comes next."

"Whaddya mean? What comes next?"

"Have you ever seen an older couple sitting at a restaurant, not talking? They're either totally comfortable with each other, or they've run out of things to say. That's terrifying to me. Walking on the moon turns into walking down the street. But don't listen to me—really don't. I'm sorry to hear about Alice."

"Yeah. I should go. I'm meeting some friends."

"You're nineteen right? Why don't you come with me to Ireland before your summer job starts?"

"Really?"

"Absolutely—you could be the first young man in history to see if

Guinness will cure a broken heart."

T looked blank.

"That was a joke. But I'm not joking about the old emerald isle—do you wanna come? I'll spill for the airfare."

"That would be cool, yeah. Thanks." I liked to see him smile. T got on his bike and pedaled down the gravel driveway.

"You'll need to bring a hat! And a jacket! It rains all the time over there!"

T turned back with a thumbs up and disappeared around the corner.

One day, when T was in fifth grade, he surprised me with a statement. He never made statements. That day, as soon as he got in the Jeep, he said, "My mom has to be my mom and my teachers have to be my teachers, but you don't have to come and see me."

My eyes welled up.

"I never thought of that," I said, barely holding my voice just above cracking. "You're right. How about backgammon at Jo Mama's and then mini-golf?"

Whatever game we played, I told him up front I wasn't going to let him win. However, I did advise him against bad moves, as a teaching tool. When he did beat me—and it usually didn't take all that long—triumph was written all over his face.

By T's junior year in high school, he was running with a pack of friends, which I expected, and I rarely saw him, and suddenly it was graduation. I hadn't seen him since I helped him move into his dorm at B.U. in January.

After T pedaled away, the scrub pines started swayed in the wind, and a light rain pattered on the roof. I hoped T would get home all right. I picked out the next letter and put my feet up on the lazy boy, with another mug of cider at hand.

Dear Rigby,   March 7, 1916

There is sad news, Rigby. George came by the shop yesterday to say that Francis is dead, from his cancer. I can't help thinking of all the stories about the Sidhe taking back the people they love, especially the artists. I still have the swan Francis whittled the day we visited Bohernabreena, and George brought with him a shiny black phonograph and a stack of records that Francis left us in his will.

I told George of your adventures with Gamal. The similarities between the solstice rituals were striking. At both Karnak and Brú na Bóinne, the sunlight is narrowed down before it enters the inner sanctum, and it falls on the water inside. That gems were part of the ritual aligns beautifully with the universal association of crystals with the travel of souls. With cause to wonder where else this rite was practiced, I remembered one of the first books I purchased from you, by Norman Lockyer, <u>The Dawn of Astronomy</u>. After George departed for the pub, I found a copy on the shelf and was reminded of why it intrigued me at the time.

On page 92: "At the spring equinox, the dawning sun shined along a passage, over the high altar at the Temple of Jerusalem, and into the holy of holies. The worshippers stood with their back to the sun, facing the priest, who stood before the altar wearing a white robe with jewels that reflected flashes and beams of color from the sun."

Page 96: Facing east, St. Peter's Basilica in Vatican City was built in 1626. On the vernal equinox, the outer and inner doors were thrown open at dawn so the rising sun would enter the church, proceed down the aisle and light up the high altar.

Considering the piles of quartz at Brú na Bóinne, more rare and valuable, clear quartz might well have been part of the ritual there. If one is going to celebrate the sun, manufacturing a rainbow would not only be visually compelling, but meaningful to people who considered it a bridge to the Other World.

I found the book of photographs from Egypt you mentioned, and gave Daniel a guided tour through all of it, over three nights, including the Temple at Karnak. He's never quite understood that his father has to be far away, and he was very excited to see the pictures. I think he felt better afterward, knowing you were in that incredible place.

In my correspondence with Mary Czaplicka, she tells me the Siberian Buryats have held spring celebrations for thousands of years to celebrate the return of the whooper swans . They tell a unique version of the swan-maiden legend, in which the swan tells her would-be captor-husband as she escapes through the smoke hole, to celebrate the swans' coming and going each year. Their primary wind instrument has a wooden neck sculpted to look like that of a swan. Mary tells me that if I were a Siberian priestess, I would have worn a long, white, swan-feather coat, with a swan's long neck arranged around my shoulders. Thus equipped with camouflage, my spiritual practice would be to live among the swans at Lake Baikal, to observe and learn.

The serialized story of Danu has been through numerous drafts, but I find the opportunity of a letter to you heightens my focus, inspiring more polish. So I take up where we left off—after making the departure of the swans each fall a musical celebration of kinship, and teaching a new and more expressive language, Danu and her followers plan to cross the unknown sea and discover the winter home of the great bird...

*   *   *   *

Finding inspiration in the graceful shape of the great bird, the Icelandic boat-builders steamed long, elegant curves in the finest wood. The long, low sides hugged the ocean waves and rode the river currents. The boat's proud breast and neck made the heavy prow stand high above the water, cutting lines of foam to either side.

Beginning their journey southeast before the Song of Flying, fifty men and women put to sea in five boats, each guided by a diviner priestess and her chieftain. Danu's boat led the way.

Following the autumn course of the swans, they would watch for the whoopers to fly over them in a day or two, so they might perfect their route.

After a day of fair wind, the sea stilled in the night, and the mariners dipped their oars in the water. To the rhythm of the rowing, the feathered priestesses sang together across the water.

To the sun's winter home flies the swan,
with old souls under wing,
to the timeless nest atop the tallest tree,
through the longest winter night,
descending in the clouds of spring,
new souls under wing.

The pre-dawn light burnt the clouds a fiery orange, a breeze blew up and a faint sound came from behind them; *whoop-ah, whoop-ah.* Dozens of swans came into view high above and flew ahead of the mariners, who set the sails and adjusted their rudders to the bird's heading.

People of the Flow

Under a steady wind, the high prows split lines of foam, rushing ahead through the day. As the moon rose, a shoreline came into view. The Icelanders rowed in and out of coves all night, and the following day, they searched the shoreline. All they observed were tall, white wolves in the hills, watching with interest.

As dusk fell, they came to the mouth of a wide tidal river surging straight inland. Following jumping salmon in the brightening moonlight, their boats rode on the tide into the deep-green country.

On the bending river, they stowed the sails and worked the oars. On the marshy banks grew yellow and purple flowers. The hills wore bright green clothes over jutting bones of granite. Creeks tumbled into rivers. The air was wet with mist.

Bats swooped and squeaked under the near-full moon. A salmon the size of a boy jumped in a boat. Comfortably browsing in the green vale were huge stags with heavy antlers. Above them on the hillsides, the tall and ghostly wolves kept pace.

As the first glow of morning lit the land, the Icelanders came to a bend in the river where they heard a sound they longed to hear—the song of the whooper swan. They rowed quickly around the bend to see hundreds of swans nesting on a marshy plain. The exhausted mariners celebrated and embraced, calling out in the way of the whooper.

Tying down at the base of a majestic hill of birch trees, they climbed to the top, looking out over the bend in the river to see hundreds of whooper swans and their massive round nests. They had discovered the winter grounds.

*   *   *   *

Rigby, I often think of us enjoying scones and tea on a Sunday afternoon after the war, growing older and sharing our days again. We will get there together, whether in Ireland or America.

Yours always,
Nessa

Chapter Eighteen

Room #204, Farris Hall, University College Dublin, May 1910

At seventy-one, Professor Richard Piggott was thin, slow-moving and deliberate. Sitting in the front row of an otherwise empty classroom, Nessa watched as he sat down, removed his handkerchief, blew his nose, re-arranged the handkerchief, put it back in his pocket, adjusted his eyeglasses, arranged his papers, dipped his pen, and made a note.

Professor Stuart Claffey was also in his declining years, but rounder than his colleague. He wore rectangular, gold-rimmed glasses and had a tuft of grey hair sprouting from each ear. Sitting between the two gentlemen was Professor Agnes O'Farrelly, the only woman on the Board of Governors of University College, Dublin. She was tall and thin with excellent posture, her greying dark hair pulled up in a bun.

"Mrs. Harrington," she said. "As you know, this is the oral exam for your thesis. It is four p.m. You may begin."

"Thank you," said Nessa, looking up from her notes. The sun shone through the window from behind the row of professors. "At best, the Celtic people are characterized in scholarship as happy warriors, and men of easy sentiment. At worst, they are lumped in

88

with the Danes, and both condemned as illiterate barbarians and buffoons. Based on extensive evidence in Celtic parables, I find these perceptions to be misguided."

A heavy cloud drifted in front of the sun. The room darkened. "If the Celts were such happy warriors, eager for cattle raids and hostage-taking, they would not have told a story in which Cuchulain, their greatest military hero, is tortured by his violent past." A few raindrops fell here and there. "Cuchulain's violent memories of war cause him to hallucinate—he sees the smoke of burning houses all around him, and for two days he fights with phantoms until he's sent off to a solitary glen in the northern forests with fifty princessses of Ulster to tend him."

"Fifty princesses," muttered Professor Piggott.

"Continue," said Professor O'Farrelly.

"Still, Cuchulain heard wild cries and wailing, the laughter of goblins, and the braying of trumpets. He saw the corpse of his wife Emer thrown from the ramparts of Emain Macha, and rode quickly back to Ulster to find her alive. She begged him to stay, but he bid her farewell, and went to his mother to tell her he wouldn't return from his next battle. He was right."

Professor Claffey sniffed and wiped his nose. A spattering rain began to fall.

"Do we speak of the same Celts that went to battle without clothing?" asked Piggott. A light rain blew against the windows.

"My thesis presupposes a cultural ethos among the Celtic people that seeks to avoid the spilling of blood and loss of treasure."

"You may continue," said Professor O'Farrelly.

"After a battle in which the hero Cuchulain slays the three sons of Nechta Scene, the hero can no longer tell the difference between friend and enemy, and he threatens to kill everyone in the Fort of Emain."

Claffey sniffed. Piggott snorted. The steady rain was louder, drumming on the roof.

"As Cuchulain approached the fort, the king sent out his queen and her consorts entirely without clothes. While distracted by their nakedness, the king's men seized Cuchulain and put him in a vat of cold water. The violent heat generated by his body breaks the first vat, and he is placed in a second, only to boil the water away. Placed in a third vat, the water merely simmers. Thus calmed, Cuchulain is admitted to the fort."

"This is self-discipline?" queried Piggott. "Naked queens and boiling cauldrons?"

The wind picked up, swaying the branches of a large oak outside the second-story classroom. The rain fell harder.

"Like so many Irish legends, the plot is fanciful and its elements exaggerated so the audience will not forget it," answered Nessa. "The underlying message is illustrated in the bones of the plot: Violent emotion is dangerous, and must be managed."

"Finding morality in this bawdy tale is akin to pulling a diamond from a donkey's arse," said Piggott.

Claffey raised his eyebrows, Nessa blushed. O'Farrelly stared at Piggott. Nessa continued.

"Perhaps the most sophisticated approach to managing heated emotions is found in the long professional tradition of the satirical poets, who traveled in groups of up to twenty-four from province to province, and were required to be sheltered and paid. Regardless of their targets, the satirist was legally protected from assault." Thunder grumbled in the distance. Claffey took a pocketknife from his vest pocket and began sharpening a pencil.

"And how do these pub-goers fit into your grand, conceptual scheme?" Piggott asked. The wind picked up outside, from whistling to howling.

"After gathering the latest news in a given town, the poets would satirize those who deserved a moral dressing down. This had the rippling effect of punishing the transgressor without real harm, while at least partially satisfying the aggrieved party or parties with a good laugh." The thunder rumbled, sounding closer.

The wind shrieked and the windows rattled. Claffey peered over his bifocal glasses at Nessa.

"Were you planning to mention that the Irish satirists lampooned no less than her majesty Queen Elizabeth, and stirred rebellion during the Williamite Wars?" The rain blew sideways on the windows.

"The international function of the satirist is outside the purview of my thesis," Nessa replied.

"Continue," said Mrs. O'Farrelly.

"Nature itself reacted against impulsive rage during the Milesian invasion of Ireland. Moments after the Milesian Captain Eber Donn exulted in brutal fury at the prospect of putting all the dwellers of Ireland to the sword, a tempest springs up and sinks his ship."

A loud clap of thunder rattled the tall classroom windows.

"It seems we have extra-curricular commentary," said O'Farrelly.

Lightning flashed.

"How dramatic. Please continue."

"When Mael Duin was bent upon avenging the murder of his father, he was, for unstated reasons, required to take his men on a long journey to find a druidic talisman."

The rain slowed. The wind lessened.

"By the time Mael returned," Mrs. O'Farrely said, "His passions were cooled and an appropriate eric fine was required. Yes, I see your point."

Piggott coughed, expectorated into his handkerchief and replaced it in his pocket. The rain pattered on the roof.

"Under the leadership of Captain Finn mac Cool, the Fianna Eireen were both army and police, protecting the ports of Ireland and the general welfare. Having learned the potential abuses of such authority, the Fianna were sworn to an ethical code that forbade them from using swaggering speech, or carping at the old, or interfering with women. Eric fines were measured in fractions of a man's wealth, so the punishment was equally painful for the rich and the poor."

The rain stopped. Piggott leaned forward and peered over his glasses at Nessa.

"Am I witness, once again, to that same, tired romantic indulgence, that abiding wish to find white knights in fantastical stories, and nothing but fault in our own traditions?"

"I have found no fault—"

"I find her arguments compelling," said O'Farrelly. "It's very sensible."

"I have mo—" began Nessa.

"I find it wanting," snapped Piggott, who stood up and gathered his books and papers. Claffey got up as well, while Piggott delivered a final broadside. "I am compelled to note that the barbarian cultures have been foolishly romanticized for a hundred years, ever since Mr. Blake made it the fashion. The romantics are less concerned with evidence and scholarship than with invented wisdom derived from backwards races." Both Piggott and Claffey left the room.

"On that delightful note, we're adjourned," said O'Farrelly, who smiled at Nessa from her seat behind the long table. "Come with me."

Out in the hallway, she put her arm around Nessa, and they walked to the stairwell.

"Don't concern yourself," she said. "I decide your final grade. My conclusion is that your thesis is compelling, and you were very impressive in defending it."

"Thank you, Mrs. O'Farrelly."

They walked down a white marble staircase to the first floor and out into the courtyard.

"I wish I could have finished."

"I'd like to hear it." They sat on a wooden bench. "Tell me."

"The legends say that after hundreds of years of costly wars and vendettas between the five provinces of Ireland, King Tuathal Teachtmhor established a *meidhe*, or neck in the first century A.D., taking a modest amount from each of the five to create a center of national unity in County Meath. The Hall of Tara was built there, from massive wooden beams." Nessa turned a page in her notebook. "It was described as 760 feet long, 90 feet wide and 45 feet high. It was the seat of the Ard-Rie, the popular king of all Ireland. He had no direct power over anyone, only the political power of his popularity."

"Yes, I'm familiar," said Professor O'Farrelly.

"Every third year, the Ard-Rie presided over a week-long gathering of provincial chiefs, who made laws as necessary and drafted new chapters in the books of genealogy and history, so no falsehoods were included. It is a model not unlike that used fifteen hundred years later in America, where Washington D.C. is the center of national unity in a pluralistic country." Nessa closed her notebook. "Yet another carefully thought out method of preventing armed conflict."

"And the games at Tailte," said Professor O'Farrelly. "They began around that time. It was a chance for champions from all the provinces to contend and compete without bloodshed." She smiled at Nessa. "Sad to say, my colleagues have as much regard for reviving the Celtic culture as they do for matriculating women here at the university, which is why, my dear Nessa, I so enjoyed both your topic, and your matching demeanor. You stood up to them like a ship in the wind, with poise and purpose." The fog in the treetops was disappearing in the afternoon sun.

Mrs. O'Farrelly stood up from the bench, as did Nessa.

"Mr. Piggott and Dr. Claffey were unnerving. I'm fortunate you were sitting between them."

"Every generation has an old guard, holding too hard to things that should be let go. Will you be in Castletownbere this summer?"

"Yes, next month."

"Please thank Miss Millington for the job she is doing, and for recommending you to University College. Will you do that?"

"I look forward to telling her everything."

Chapter Nineteen

Middle Abbey St., Dublin, April 30, 2009

"Taking off was cool—getting pushed back in the seat like that—but I'm not so sure about the landing, I don't know."

I'd just woken up, and we were ten minutes out of Dublin Airport. T's face looked like we were about to fly straight into a mountain. I took out the book Melissa gave me for a buy-out present, Standish O'Grady's *History of Ireland*.

"Check this out, T—there was a queen Nessa like a thousand years ago. Her son Concobar became king. You know what they called him?"

"Concobar the king?"

"Concobar mac Nessa."

"Yeah?"

"It wasn't Concobar, son of whoever his father was. It was Concobar, son of Nessa."

"Because she was the queen?"

"Let's say they placed a higher value on women than some cultures I can think of."

T's face was still pale and sweaty.

"Seatbelts on," said the passing flight attendant. "Tray tables to their upright position."

"T, this is weird. Check this out. There's a battle between the Fomorians and the Tuatha Dé Danann, and the Fomorians have this weapon called Balor's Eye, which took nine men with hooks to open, and its very glance turned people to stone." T looked at me like I was crazy, but I had his attention.

"But their hero, Lugh of the Long Throw, casts a stone at Balor's Eye and smashes it, and the Fomorians are driven out of Ireland."

Looking past T, out the widow behind him, I could see the ground approaching.

"What are you talking about?" asked T. That's when the airplane tires made that little landing noise, and the plane lurched, bouncing a little back and forth, and then settling onto the runway.

"Damn," said T.

"We're here. The land where Balor's Eye got squished."

That got a tired smile from T.

Landing at four thirty-eight a.m., we caught a cab to Middle Abbey Street in downtown Dublin, which was deserted but for the occasional young couple leaving the late night dance clubs. More importantly, our destination wasn't a hotel, it was Dublin Apartments I, and the front door was locked. All I had was a name, Nancy, and a phone number. I checked my phone and found a text from the day before: It was Nancy, wanting to know when we'd be arriving. T was tapping his feet.

There's always a ball that drops in the final rush of organizing a trip. I sat on the stoop. T sat next to me. The last of the late night clubs was letting out down the street.

"I'd forgotten how damp the air is here." I sniffed. "Three thousand miles of cold spray and wind all heading east across the Atlantic at great speeds, at all times, rolling over the hills of Ireland and whistling at the sheep."

"Is this part of the tour?" asked T.

A young man with a buzzcut and an earring walked by, smoking a cigarette.

I sighed.

"There's someone named Nancy sleeping peacefully nearby who I don't wish to wake up at this hour, specifically because it's not her fault that I only just read the text she sent yesterday regarding when she might expect us."

"Hm."

T hopped back and forth to keep warm. I got out the knapsack and took out the wood box. I opened it and got out the black and white photograph of Rigby, Nessa and George Russell in front of the Entrance Stone at Brú na Bóinne. I pointed them out.

"Rigby sort of looks like you."

I looked at the picture again. "Maybe."

I put it back in the wood box, took a book from my backpack and handed it to T.

"Read the outlined part at the book mark." T gave me a funny look. "It's just a few sentences."

He took the book and stepped closer to the overhead streetlight. "I am Aengus; men call me the young," he began, "I am the sunlight in the heart, the moonlight in the mind, I am the light at the end of every dream, the voice forever calling to come away. I am the desire beyond joy and tears." T looked up. "What *is* this?"

"The Irish poet George Russell. He's the big guy with Ness and Rigby in the picture. He said he was lying on the mound when wild words came flying into his head. They called the mound by its Gaelic name, Brú na Bóinne—house on the river."

"What was all that stuff about voices calling?"

"Old George saw Brú na Bóinne as a portal, a gateway to Tír na nÓg, the timeless Irish heaven where birds sing, music plays and everything is copacetic."

"Like Stargate?"

"The movie?"

"Or the series."

"Not like Stargate. No computerized wormholes that I know of."

"So how do you get to the other side? Where's the gate?"

"That's the big question. I suspect it's more of a mental thing, a state of mind.

Maybe you can figure it out."

"Me?"

"Good as anyone. We're goin' to see it tomorrow."

"Nice."

T stopped swaying back and forth. He got out his phone and typed.

"Look up Newgrange, that's the English word for the place."

T typed, scrolled down, typed some more.

"UNESCO site, hmmm…" Tap, tap. "The mound at Newgrange is two-hundred and thirty-five feet in diameter and thirty feet high." Tap, tap, tap. "There's a sixty foot passage to a domed central chamber, built circa 3,200 B.C., by peoples unknown."

"Five hundred years older than the first pyramid," I added, as a drunken couple staggered by.

"Really?"

"Every year about 30,000 people enter a lottery to be in the central chamber at dawn on the winter solstice, when the sun comes down the passage and into the chamber."

"Nobody knows who built it?"

"Nope." I rummaged in my backpack. "Want a cookie?"

We both had two sugar cookies washed down with water, after which T started hopping back and forth again. He didn't seem upset, just a bit chilly. I checked my watch and decided that calling Nancy at six-fifteen a.m. was within the outer realm of civilized behavior. A sleepy female voice answered and gave me the code to open the door. I typed it in, and we were inside. Nice and warm.

"Your apartment's in the building around the corner, and you'll need keys," said the sleepy voice. "Open the closet behind the front door and look for a key dangling from a nail at about knee-height on the left."

It was an old-fashioned skeleton key.

"Got it."

"The key opens the closet under the stairs—it's sort of a security center and there's a box of keys on the desk."

I found the box, which was full of keys.

"Got the box of keys."

I handed T the box.

"I find the best thing is just dump 'em on the floor and look for the one that says Inside Rooms."

Hearing Nancy's voice from the phone, T followed her directions and soon had the key. Nancy suggested we sleep for a bit and she'd be around at nine-thirty or so. I thanked her profusely and hung up.

"That was a little weird," said T. "I mean, as a system."

"Let me tell ya somethin'. The Ireland I know and love is a place where good enough is good enough."

Inside the apartment, T collapsed on a bed, and was asleep before I could suggest taking his shoes off. I was still wired. There was something about crossing the Atlantic in a giant metal flying machine that was always unnerving. It didn't seem believable. I found some hot chocolate mix with little marshmallows, and fixed up a cup. Sitting at the kitchen table, I was careful not to spill hot chocolate on the next letter.

My lovely Nessa,   March 29, 1916

You have just taken this letter from a blue envelope, which designates that an officer has sworn the letter inside contains nothing treasonous, seditious or otherwise outside the bounds of military protocol.

The blue envelopes are a response to the annoyance and/or personal discomfort regimental officers have with regard to spending their valuable time poring over their buddy's letter home to Ma. Swear on the blue envelope, and we can move on with the war. My opportunity to 'speak freely' in present company is limited to this letter, the writing of which will be of therapeutic benefit to my worn psyche.

As you know, I wasn't one who celebrated the coming of war, but perceived it as a necessary response to aggression. Now I see it as a bloody house of cards. The maze of alliances formed from colonial expansion has conjured up a war that spreads across continents like an infernal disease.

Aussies and Kiwis traveled thousands of miles to fight the Turks, who never caused them offense. While it is admirable for such far-flung British subjects to demonstrate their loyalty, the effort was doomed to failure. Who will fight harder and more effectively? Those who travel far from their homes and have no direct argument with the enemy, or those who are defending their own land?

I traveled to Anzac Cove on a supply ship last month. The high cliffs could not be more perfectly positioned for defensive purposes. I witnessed the pulverized remains of landing craft annihilated by Turkish shells before they could reach shore. That tens of thousands were sent to their deaths can only be laid at the feet of righteous pride and stubborn foolishness. I was told that as the evacuation finally began, the Turks ceased their shelling. They would have been within their rights to continue the bombardment, yet they stood by. It was an act of decency.

Where in the past there was a sense of nobility in the sweep of the cavalry, the tailored uniforms and skilled swordsmen, now the Germans kill thousands with mustard gas at Ypres. No one is prepared for what is unfolding, and no one can stop the runaway train. From the Crow's Nest, I see men and ships bristling with mechanized modern armaments that promise instant destruction. The track and pipeline are progressing.

Your story of the Tuatha Dé Danann in Iceland and their arrival in Ireland is an elegant and imaginative way of filling in a lost hapter in the shrouded history of Eire.

I think often and fondly of our adventures at Brú na Bóinne, first with George, and then just the two of us. I miss you and Daniel every day.

Yours always,
Rigby

Chapter Twenty

The townland of Disert, County Cork, July 1912

George Russell's bushy, red beard hovered over the chess pieces. Nessa sat opposite, smiling. Rigby perched nearby on the edge of an oak table, with his pipe. George slid his bishop halfway across the board.

"Why?" said Nessa. "Why do you seek out certain death?"

"'Tis a noble bishop, striding onto the field of play," George boomed.

"And into the shadows of the valley of death," said Nessa, taking his bishop with her knight.

"'Tis nothing," said George, scooping gooey brie onto a pair of crackers. "The holy bishop shall rise on judgment day." Bits of cracker lodged in his beard as he ate. He took a pull of homemade ale.

"How's the new batch?" said Rigby, puffing on his pipe.

"Thick as molasses and twice as tasty," said George, moving a pawn diagonal to Nessa's knight.

"I'll have one, I think, to fortify me for the trip," said Rigby. "Nessa?"

"Chocolate ice cream please, with milk and rum."

George lifted an eyebrow, as Rigby went off to the kitchen. Nessa took George's pawn with her knight.

"Check."

"My noble king," said George, slumping in his chair. "Assailed by villains."

George moved his king to temporary safety. Nessa's knight took George's queen. George's king took Nessa's knight.

"The villain is dispatched by the slow yet effective king," said George, taking a deep drought of homemade brew. "Aaah, that's good!"

Rigby returned with the drinks and observed the board.

"Another slaughter," said Rigby. Nessa slid her bishop from behind her pawns.

"Mmm," said George. "A feelin' of imminent doom settles over the king. He must find safe harbor."

Nessa sampled her ice cream and rum concoction with a spoon. In three moves, the match was over.

"Checkmate," said Nessa.

"Assassin!" said George. "I am slain! The regal blood gushes forth, staining the royal robe. I am left only to hope that my deeds of honor will be spoken of at great banquets, by my adoring descendants." Rigby sipped his drink and puffed his pipe. There was a knock on the front door.

"That's Da," said Nessa, getting up from her chair. Rigby opened the door and Nessa gave her Da a hug.

"Thank you for bringin' the horses. Ma's upstairs with Daniel."

Gerald led Nessa onto the front porch.

"I was talkin' with Fergus at the livery and a familiar lady comes along. We get to talkin' and right off she's interested in our little sojourn, and I asked her to come along. I believe you know her."

Nessa looked down the path as a brown and white pony approached, with a roundish woman riding side-saddle. Nessa recognized the loose bun just to the side of her head. Miss Millington. Nessa went to greet her.

"It's wonderful to see you," said Nessa. "I should have thought to invite you myself."

With his thick red moustache and overflowing beard preceding him, George came down the steps.

"I was just going for my Saturday ride, but from what Gerald tells me, your little adventure sounds much better," said Miss Millington, her voice trailing off as George gazed at her sweetly.

"George Russell, this is Miss Millington," said Nessa. "She started a library for the Gaelic League in Castletownbere when I was a little girl."

"Please call me Jo, or Johannah if you must," said Miss Millington.

George kneeled down before her and took her hand.

"A savior of Erin," he said, still wearing bits of white cracker in his beard. "Guardian of treasures, keeper of wonders, teller of tales."

George slowly stood, and embraced the somewhat reluctant Miss Millington. He turned to Gerald.

"You met her on the livery? I say there is no coincidence! She was *meant* to come along."

Miss Millington smiled as George helped her back onto the pony. Nessa tucked her rust-colored wool pants inside black leather boots, arranged her red-orange hair under a black riding helmet, and was up on her chestnut brown horse. Nessa slowly led the way up the ridge behind the house while Gerald and George finished loading the pack-horse.

"When I wasn't at the library, I was up in these hills," said Nessa.

"It's beautiful," said Miss Millington. "I've never been out this way."

Halfway up the grassy granite pile, the wind picked up, and they stopped to take in the first view of the ocean. Sitting straight and tall in the saddle, Rigby came up behind them.

"I love cantering on the beach, but it's some ways north before there's a long enough stretch," said Nessa. "I must have been on that stretch of beach half a dozen times before I noticed something flash in the sun near the top of the cliff. The next time out I saw the flash again, and found a long way 'round the back side to the top."

Nessa and Johannah started the horses again, at a walk up the rocky path. Rigby moved ahead of them.

"What did you find?" asked Miss Millington.

"There's a lot of pitch pine and rose hip bushes up there, but finally it opened into a small area where it's mostly sand and grass. That's where I found the cairn."

They cleared the first ridge with George and Gerald catching up. On the far side was a narrow, pasture sloping downward, lined with a low stone wall. The horses picked their way through the rough field.

"The cairn was made of white quartz stones, smooth all 'round like a river rock, and there were more scattered all around."

Nessa removed a smooth, oval-shaped white stone from a pocket in her saddle, about the size of a potato. She handed it to Johannah. "I kept one."

Rigby's horse defecated as it walked. Nessa rolled her eyes and held her breath while Johannah pressed a handkerchief to her face. They plodded on.

"The next year I was in Dublin, and visited Brú na Bóinne with Rigby and George, and the same stones were everywhere. Stewart Macalister is the archeologist working there, and he says the mound might have originally been covered with quartz. Rigby!"

Rigby let Nessa and Miss Millington catch up.

"When does McAlister say the Bru was built?" Nessa asked him.

"About 2,500 B.C., almost surely before the Celtic people ever got to Ireland." Rigby tamped his pipe, letting the two women past.

"Whoever built the Bru stripped a great deal of turf to do it," said Nessa. "Which reminded me of the entry for the place-name Disert in Cormac's Glossary, which says, 'Though barren now, a great house was there before.' And there's a note saying the word stripped could be used interchangeably with the word barren."

"Disert, as in deserted," said Miss Millington. "Barren could mean stripped of turf. Your cairn was in a sandy area." Rigby caught up with the two women.

"English monks prefer a large building with many little rooms," said Rigby. "The Irish preferred little cottages in remote places. It would be no surprise if there are remains of a hermitage along the coast."

"I'd be surprised if there weren't," said Johannah.

After an hour on the trail, Nessa led the way to a high pasture, where Rigby helped Gerald unpack the food and beverages, while George helped Jo arrange the blankets inside the high side of the pasture's stone wall, out of the wind.

"It's game trails from here on," said Nessa, settling down with a slab of brown bread, butter and honey. George turned the smooth quartz stone in his hands.

"What's the meaning, George?" asked Rigby, cutting himself a hunk of cheddar. "Why is there always quartz at ancient temples? Lockyer says the Great Pyramid originally had a quartz capstone."

"Crystals are seeds from the stars," said George turning the stone in the sunlight. "They both sparkle. The Pawnee say that Evening Star sent Mother Corn to earth on a cloud."

"Quartz retains heat more efficiently than a more porous stone," said Rigby, slicing an apple. "It would radiate heat for a longer period of time."

Rigby put slices of apple and cheese on a cracker, and handed it to Johannah.

"Thank you," she said. "On Bearhaven Island, I met a family that still heats their milk with hot stones rather than over the fire. I don't know if they use quartz."

"There are dozens of fire pits at Brú na Bóinne," said Nessa. "They might have used them to heat stones. They could have heated the shallow pool in front, or brought them inside, to the basin."

"They found an antler inside the Brú when it was discovered in 1699," said Rigby, lighting his pipe. "They could have used an antler to move the hot stones. Part of the ceremony."

"Or a stag wandered inside, was trapped and died," said Gerald, finishing off a brown bottle of homemade ale. "Leaving, after a few thousand years, only its antlers." He got up.

"The voice of reason," said Nessa, smiling at her Da.

She washed an apple with water from her canteen.

"Nessa's right," said George. "If they filled the basins with water from the internal spring and then dropped the glowing hot quartz stones in the water…. whooosshh." George threw up his hands like a magician.

"A steam-bath," said Rigby, tamping his pipe. "It's the oldest pastime in human history."

"And utterly dark inside the chamber," said Nessa, finishing off the apple. "Like the Indian sweat lodge."

"Deprived of sight, one looks inward," said George. "Deprived of food, one has visions. The legends say people came to fast for days at Brú na Bóinne, to open a gateway to the other world."

The rush of talk stopped for a moment.

"Let's go," said George.

Half an hour later, the sun was halfway down the sky, and everyone heard the sharp snap of the pony's ankle. Johannah fell to the ground and rolled over. The pony shrieked. Gerald dismounted with his rifle and went to Johannah, who was watching the pony scream and twist on the ground. Nessa dismounted and stood with Johannah. Gerald jacked a shell into his rifle and shot the pony in the head.

"I'm so sorry," said Miss Millington.

"Not your fault," said Gerald, getting up on his horse.

Soon they emerged out of the wind-twisted pitch pine and clinging rose hip bushes into a high clearing on the cliff top. Smooth white stones littered the sandy ground. Clumps of grass took hold every few feet. They tied the horses to the pines at the edge of the clearing, and quietly approached the small pile of quartz near the center of it. Johannah walked over to Gerald and whispered something in his ear. He nodded, and they both walked over to the cairn.

"After I saw that flash, I brought my binoculars to the beach, and up near the top of the cliff there was a cave, where the flash was," said Nessa. "It must be somewhere below us, but the cliff is sheer."

George kneeled at the cairn, muttered a few words and began dismantling it. Rigby joined him until the stones were scattered. They scooped away sand and pebbles until a cloud of dust drifted upwards and was snatched away by the wind. George stood up. Rigby patted dust off his back.

Gerald picked up a sturdy branch, almost long enough for a walking stick, and poked at the ground near the cairn.

"All right then," said Rigby. "Get your sticks and form a line."

George, Nessa and Jo followed Rigby to the edge of the clearing, picked out their sticks, made a line and began poking at the ground. Making their way slowly across the sandy clearing, Nessa's stick fell into a hole. She looked closer and a greenish snake slipped out, quickly disappearing across the sand and into the bushes.

108

After ten minutes, they reached the end of the clearing. "Back again," said Rigby. They re-formed the line with some grumbling and poking of each other, and resumed testing the ground. A pair of rabbits shot past Rigby's feet.

Jo's stick tapped on a rock. She tapped a foot further, still hitting the rock, a few inches under the sand. Coming up next to Jo, Nessa's stick clicked on the same rock. It was big and flat. Kneeling and squatting around the edges, they cleared away the sand. It was oval-shaped, a cut slab of grey granite, shot through with faint pink veins of quartz. They dug around the edges of the flat stone. It was only three inches thick. No one spoke. Seagulls wheeled overhead.

Gerald and George knelt down and pushed at the edge together. The stone slid a few inches, revealing blackness below. They pushed again. The grey slab slid aside onto the sand. Gerald stood and wiped his brow.

"Well now," said George. "What have we here?"

He kneeled down and peered down the round hole, about three feet across.

"Can't see the bottom of the hole."

Rigby retrieved a rope and flashlights from the pack-horse. Gerald tied a stone to the end of the rope and lowered it into the dark hole until it went slack. He pulled up the rope and examined the length. "There's some kind of floor about six feet down."

Rigby wound the rope around a granite boulder and tied a knot, paying the rest down the hole.

"Gerald, I'd say your frame would have one hell of a time in that hole, and George is even bigger," said Rigby. "And no matter how much I love my wife's sense of daring and adventure, I can't exactly stand by and watch her go down a dark hole inside a five hundred foot cliff, nor would I stand to see the town librarian go the same way, and finally, I had the lightest lunch."

Nessa handed him the rope.

"Once again, my dear, your reasoning is overwhelming," she said. "Hold on tight."

Rigby backed into the hole, and slid slowly down until the top of his head was just below the top of the hole.

"There's a tunnel," he said. "I think I can fit." Rigby disappeared and Nessa took the rope, backing her way into the hole. Seeing the tunnel, she followed Rigby's feet. It was wide enough to wriggle four or five inches at a time. With each breath, she felt her ribcage against the walls. Rigby's feet disappeared. She heard a faint voice.

"Oh, my god." It was Rigby.

Nessa wriggled forward and didn't stop pushing with her legs until she came to the opening. Rigby helped her out into a round cave, about twenty feet across. The floor was sandy, littered with smooth quartz stones. Through the cave opening was sky and ocean. Nessa felt the wind fluttering, and heard gulls calling. Rigby turned on his flashlight, illuminating the back of the cave. A pile of smooth quartz stones was carefully stacked against the back wall. Resting on top of the stones was the remains of a large, white wing, still holding some of its feathers. Beneath it was the skeleton of a small child.

Nessa knelt down. She saw feathers at her feet. Rigby knelt beside her. She closed her eyes. The wind picked up, shifting her hair. She stood and looked at the child's skeleton. Rigby stood behind her. There were pieces of clear crystal quartz in the eye sockets. A third clear crystal lay at its feet.

Nessa turned and moved to the cave opening. Far below, the beach was empty. Tall waves slumped onto the rocks jutting into the ocean. In the distance, a fishing boat bobbed on the waves.

"We should tell the others," said Nessa.

"Tell them what?"

Nessa smiled. There were tears on her cheeks.

"Hallooo!"

The voice came from the passage. Rigby helped Johannah into the cave. The sounds of talk and moving feet echoed slightly in the cave. Then it was quiet. Johannah gazed at the wing arranged over the child's skeleton.

"I..." After a moment, she turned away and flicked on her flashlight. They all began to scan the walls. On the grey granite in the darker side of the cave was a spiral etched in the stone, then another below it, and a third below that.

Nessa tripped and almost fell. She knelt down and cleared sand away to find a small hole inset in the floor, oval in shape, about three inches long and deep. It had been cut out with a tool. It was empty.

A spider crawled over Rigby's hand and down his arm. He flicked it away, and watched it crawl into a dark corner. He aimed his flashlight at the retreating spider. It scrambled over a battered wooden box. Rigby walked over and picked it up. Inside were shreds of what seemed like paper. Some of the edges were brown. He felt a piece in his hand. It wasn't paper. It was vellum. Rigby knew the feel from the semester he'd spent with ancient manuscripts at Oxford. He put the box in his knapsack.

The cave darkened as the sun slipped behind a bank of clouds on the horizon. They set up camp in the clearing as the moon rose, eating and drinking and tending the fire. They talked of the Tuatha Dé Danann, who came rolling out of a sea fog on three-spoked wheels, to the strains of a traveling song.

They talked of the local hero, Geoffrey Keating, who was descended from the last pagan king, Dathi of North Connacht— Keating broke out of Cromwell's jail in Cork City, an outlaw on the run, riding from castle to glen, saving ancient manuscripts from English torches, and writing down his own history of Ireland by moonlight along the way, including the story of Ceasair and Fintann, who landed in Dunmare, not far away.

"When refused a place on the ark," boomed George, "Ceasair and Fintann abandoned the god of Noah, made their own idols and built their own boat, landin' finally after a great gale in the harbor at Dun na m-barc, in the district of Corca Dhuibhne, and their line still runs in these hills."

Rigby stood up and offered a toast.

"To King Edward III, who five hundred years ago ordered the sheriff of Kilkenny to jail any native Englishman who spoke Gaelic, and to forbid them from having their children nurse amongst the Irish."

"How'd that work out?" asked Gerald.

"Two centuries later, the Dublin Parliament did all their business in Gaelic, and according to Irish custom."

"We swallowed the Normans and we swallowed the Danes," said Gerald, holding up his glass.

They talked of faeries, and why the little people dance in a circle, and why, if you join them, you should be very sure not to miss a step. Finally, filled to the brim with ale, Rigby, George, Jo, Nessa and Gerald held hands in a circle and danced around the fire, their heads thrown back, goin' faster and faster, the stars blurring in the sky.

Nessa heard her heart beating and saw her feet moving, but felt nothing below her. In her ears were singing voices and a symphony of rushing water. The turning stars were a streak of churning milk. She floated upward on stairs of wind and notes. Finally the circle slowed, and their hands fell apart. George staggered and fell. Nessa sat on the sandy ground. Rigby sat next to her.

Before dawn, Rigby and Nessa quietly emerged from their tent, slipped down the hole, wriggled through the tunnel and came out in the dark cave. Nessa knelt at the foot of the skeleton and said a prayer to its soul. She stood and removed the clear quartz crystal laying at the skeleton's feet. As Rigby trained his flashlight on the small oval hole cut in the cave floor, Nessa placed the crystal in the inset and filled it with water from a canteen.

They sat together against the cave wall, Rigby's arm around Nessa. Soon an ambient glow filled the cave. A few minutes later, a sunbeam entered, half cut off by a jutting rock, lighting the top of the cave wall. Slowly descending, the sun lit up one of the spirals, then slowly moved down to shine on the second, and the third.

Moving steadily across the floor, sunbeams reached the oval inset, flashing colors off the clear crystal and sparkling in the water. The moment passed, and the sunlight withdrew steadily toward the mouth of the cave, and disappeared.

Chapter Twenty-one

Downtown Dublin, April 30, 2009

It was just warm enough to sit outside at Searsons Bar on Baggot Street. T pointed out that, according to mapquest, we were on Maggot Street.

Dr. Patrick Claffey had described himself as an older man of average height with white hair and a cane. He was already five minutes late. T was busy with his smartphone.

"The weather tomorrow says *cloudy with spotty showers*, and for Thursday it says *periods of rain and mostly cloudy*, and Friday it says *a little rain in the morning and showers in the afternoon*."

"What about Saturday?"

"*Rather cloudy with a stray shower*."

"You know it's Ireland when there's twenty ways to say it's rainin'."

T smiled. "Is it ever sunny?"

"Only in the imagination." I was enjoying my role as enigmatic tour guide when an older man with a cane walked up. I introduced myself and T, and we went inside. Dr. Claffey knew all the waitresses. I'd emailed him at the Geneological Records Foundation before leaving the States and offered a free lunch at his favorite restaurant if he could help me get any further with Rigby and Ness.

We sat at a marble table with fine cutlery and white cloth napkins. T and I ordered fish and chips and iced tea. Dr. Claffey ordered salmon and a pint of Guinness.

"Dr. Claffey—"

"The name's Patrick."

"This is a beautiful place, " I said. "So, I imagine you get a lot of people searching through the branches of their family tree."

"Not many enterprising enough to offer a free lunch." The waitress brought the Guinness, and Patrick took a healthy swallow.

"I noticed the giant spire on O'Connell Street," I said. "Not sure I like it much."

"No one does. It was supposed to be part of the millennium celebration."

"What happened?" asked T.

"It wasn't finished until 2003."

"Good enough," said T. I smiled to myself. Good to know he was paying
attention.

"So," I said, "My great-grandparents." The food arrived. After washing down the salmon with a draw from the pint, Patrick wiped his beard.

"Rigby Harrington enlisted in the British Army Service Corps in 1915, was stationed at El Kantara, Egypt, and deserted in June 1916. No trace of him after. I checked the passenger lists, but couldn't find a Harold who was the right age. He could have given the wrong age. He could have stowed away. I pulled out all the usual stops but came up empty. Sorry, lad." He started back in on the salmon.

"And Nessa?"

Patrick chewed carefully and nodded his head from side to side. He took another draw on the pint, and wiped his beard. The glass was empty. I waved for another.

"Nessa Ó Dálaigh Harrington. Born in the Townland of Disert, County Cork, 1888. Married Rigby Harrington in Dublin January 1911, was graduated from University College Dublin in June the same year, gave birth to Daniel in September. Busy year for Ness. Searched all the counties, couldn't find a death record. Searched all the ships. She never emigrated." The second pint arrived. "Thanks dear." Patrick took the foam and two inches off the top. "Aahh. Unusual name, Ness. So I looked for her son Daniel, and he shows up back in Disart, getting married and so forth, but I imagine you know that part." He was almost finished with the salmon.

"How unusual is not finding a death record?"

He nodded his head back and forth, chewed and swallowed.

"Fairly unusual. Rather odd. The parish priests were *very careful*—did ya know the marriage certificates used to ask if the bride and groom were first, second or third cousins? That's a how do-you-do."

"What could have happened to her?"

"I don't know. If she died and was buried, it wasn't under the auspices of a parish priest." I called for the check.

"Have ya been to Hyannisport to see the museum?" Patrick asked.

"Yes."

"I still remember when President Kennedy came to Ireland in 1963. I was in the crowd, eleven years old. There was never a turnout such as that in Dublin before...or since. It was a beautiful day..."

I paid the check and we all shook hands.

"One last thing Patrick," I said. "What do you know about the Tuatha Dé Danann?"

"Our records don't go that far back." He smiled and winked and drained his glass.

Chapter Twenty-two

St. Mary's Church, Haddington Road, Dublin October 31, 1911

Rigby held an umbrella over Ness as they got out of the carriage in front of St. Mary's. Behind them were Gerald and Mary, who held a well-wrapped Daniel in her arms.

At one hundred and sixty-eight feet, the top of the limestone bell tower disappeared into the fog above them. A pale young priest opened the iron gate to the street and led the party around to the side door.

"I'm not allowed back in the front door yet," Ness whispered to Rigby. "I must go 'round the side to beg entrance."

"It's up to you, Ness," whispered Rigby. "I'm with you, staying or going."

"It'll make Mum happy, and it'll make Da's life easier."

Ness took a deep breath as the priest opened the side door to the church. She thought of Boann, the Tuatha Dé Danann goddess who taught the skills of champions to the standing police known as the *Fianna Eireen*.

An older priest stood in the hallway in front of a set of tall wooden doors that led to the side of the altar. The doors were closed. The priest crossed himself and held his palms up to the sky.

"In the name of the Father, and of the Son, and of the Holy

Spirit." The priest made the sign of the cross, opened his prayer book and turned to Ness. "May Christ, who became one of us in the womb of the Virgin Mary, be with you. The Christian community has already welcomed with joy the child you have borne and in the celebration of his baptism has prayed that you will fully recognize the gift you have received and the responsibility entrusted to you in the Church and that, like Mary, you will proclaim the greatness of the Lord. Today, we all wish to join with you in glad thanksgiving as we call on God to bless you."

The priest's voice echoed into silence in the long hall.

The priest mouthed the word "Amen" to Ness.

"Boann," said Ness.

The priest stared over his glasses at Ness. He opened the prayer book.

"Happy are you who fear the Lord, who walk in his ways. For you shall eat the fruit of your handiwork; happy shall you be, and favored. Your wife shall be like a fruitful vine in the recesses of your home; your children like olive plants around your table."

The priest turned and opened the side doors to the nave. Gerald ushered the group inside to the pews. Ness stood just outside the doors. Rigby took her hand and whispered in her ear.

"Are we proceeding?"

"I prefer the company of Boann," said Ness quietly, "the strong and swift, the musical, the witty and radiant, the dancing and joyful Boann, thirsty for everlasting truth. Not Mary the quiet, the speechless, the obedient."

"I don't disagree. But here we are."

"You do remember where Daniel was conceived."

"As if it were yesterday."

Ness smiled, and they walked in to the nave and sat down in the front pew. The priest opened his songbook to the Canticle of Mary.

Chapter Twenty-three

Mound at Newgrange, UNESCO site, May 1, 2009

"Did you say this place was a sauna?" whispered T.

"That's what Rigby and Nessa thought."

We were inside the central chamber with several other tourists, listening to the tour guide, Shelly, a petite brunette with a smart uniform. There were spirals, hatched triangles and waves etched in most of the stones.

An elderly man whispered to his wife in German, as Shelly happily explained how the Neolithic builders created the corbelled dome by stacking the slabs so each one stuck out a bit further than the one below it.

"And every year, more than 30,000 people sign up for a lottery to be in this chamber at dawn on the winter solstice," said Shelly, with a touch of dramatic wonder in her voice. "Only ten are selected. We have videos of the solstice in the visitor center."

I felt a tap on my shoulder. "She hasn't said anything about a sauna," whispered T. "She keeps calling it a passage tomb."

I waited for a pause from Shelly.

"Excuse me," I said, holding up my hand. "Why do they call it a passage tomb if, from what I understand, no one is buried here?"

"Bones and artifacts were found that suggest it was used for funerary purposes. There are hundreds of passage tombs all over Ireland."

"But those are much smaller," I said. "Nowhere near this big."

"That's right," said Shelly.

"Was zere a skeleton here, or more zan one?" asked the elderly German man.

"No skeletons, just bits of bone—some were found in the basin," said Shelly, smiling.

A voice came from next to me. "Why call it a tomb when no one's buried here?" asked T.

"We have books on the archeological study of Newgrange in the visitor's center," said Shelly, her voice less bubbly. "We have only about five minutes before the next group."

At the back of the chamber, opposite the passage, three spirals elegantly linked together on a massive stone. The inside of the granite basin was smoother than I imagined, and the arc of its curve was perfect.

"Shelly said the basin inside the mound at Dowth is wider than the passage," whispered T. "No one could ever steal it."

"Pretty smart."

We gazed at more weird waves and spirals, until Shelly led us out through the sixty-foot passage. T and I had to hunch down slightly all the way, before emerging into a sunny afternoon. "Please be at the bus in ten minutes!" said Shelly.

T and I walked up a path to the top of the mound. The countryside spread out everywhere, cows dotting the pastures.

"That was funny when the tour bus had to stop for the cows," said T.

"Never seen that huh?"

"Nope."

I got two oranges from my knapsack and tossed one to T.

"You still think it's a sauna?" he asked.

120

I started peeling the orange.

"Yup."

The elderly German couple appeared at the top of the path.

"Hallo!" said the man, tall and fit with short, white hair. "I am Karl." We introduced ourselves. His wife Gerta was just a few inches shorter, with curly blonde hair.

"Gerta read six books before we came." Gerta spoke a few words to him in German. "In winter solstice celebrating, it is birzday of ze sun, first day of year for sun, not for death."

"There are a lot of different theories," I said, speaking more slowly and clearly than usual. "Some say it's a temple, like a church—a place to celebrate birth, marriage, and death. They say the acoustics are tremendous inside the chamber, which says they made music inside."

Karl translated for Gerta, who took a book from her bag, flipped through and found the page she wanted. She gave the book to Karl, and pointed to the passage.

"From tenth century, she says." Karl looked at the cover. "*The Dindsenchas.*" He read haltingly. "Behold ze bed of Dagda who paid noble court after the chase to a fair woman free from age and sorrow. Behold ze two paps of his consort, here beyond ze mound, vest of ze fairy mansion, where Cermait was born. Behold it there, not a far step."

Gerta was looking west, beaming into the setting sun and pink-colored clouds. Where she was looking, I noticed two grassy mounds about fifty yards away. They weren't far apart, and each was about a third the size of the mound we stood on. "Ze paps," said Gerta, cupping her breasts and smiling. I smiled back, nodding.

"Time for the bus," said Karl, pointing. The tour guide was waving from below. T and I followed Karl and Gerta down the curving path on the side of the mound.

"If those two mounds out there were, um, paps," said T. "Then this mound…" He paused.

"…is the womb," I said.
"Gerta doesn't think it's about death either," said T.
"Nope."

Chapter Twenty-four

12:20 p.m. Downtown Dublin, April 24, 1916

With Daniel's help, Nessa was cleaning the front windows of Harrington's Booksellers when three men bicycled past wearing ammunition belts strapped across their chests.

Then a group of four walked by in the uniform of the Irish Citizen Army, with pistol belts and rifles. Nessa waved down an older man on a bicycle and asked him what was happening.

"It's rebellion weather," he said. "Take the boy home." He cycled away. The week before, George had said to expect some kind of disruption at the Easter Sunday parade. Nessa and Daniel attended but saw nothing out of the ordinary.

Monday morning felt different. Another wave of men with rifles and pistols passed by, walking and riding bicycles. They were heading toward Liberty Hall. Nessa had donated vegetables and volunteered there with Daniel. Liberty Hall was also home to *The Worker's Republic* newspaper, along with a modest munitions factory for the Citizen Army.

As Nessa finished rinsing off the shop windows, George appeared on a bicycle.

"Where's your bandolier?" asked Nessa.

"My sword is my pen," said George. "Right now, I'd like

nothin' more than to bring you and young Daniel home. All this could be more high drama than tragedy, but there's no tellin' for sure." George bent down to his level. "What say you and your Ma take Monday off from work?"

Daniel smiled.

Nessa sighed. "If people only spent more time browsing peacefully in their local bookstores…"

"Not today," said George. "If I'm readin' the weather right, and I usually do, the soup's comin' to boil, and your shop is too close to the kitchen."

Nessa poured the soapy water out into the street, put the bucket and rags inside, and locked the front door. She took Daniel's hand, while George walked his bicycle away from Tara Street and the Liffey, away from Liberty Hall.

"This has been coming for a long time," said George. "When young people have no hope and see no future, they'll fight for their lives, because they have none."

Nessa prevailed on George to stop at the post office before escorting her and Daniel north of the downtown to their neighborhood in Drumcondra. After picking up her mail, Nessa, Daniel, and George were walking down the steps of the post office when dozens of armed men in the green uniform of the Irish Citizen Army ran by them and into the building. They wore slouch hats, with one side rakishly pinned up, like the pictures of Theodore Roosevelt at San Juan Hill.

Nessa squeezed Daniel's hand and kept walking away with George, as armed men flooded up the steps. Across the street, the trio hurried into a tobacco shop, where most of the patrons were gathered near the windows. George bought a cigar, lit it, and stood on a chair for a better view.

"I fail to see the strategic military value of taking the General Post Office," he said. "Even if they take out the telephone system as well, the Limeys have two-way radios now."

A group of citizen soldiers emerged from the front doors of

the post office with rifles. Behind them came a smaller group without uniforms. Nessa saw a woman take out a scroll on the post office steps and begin to read. Much of the crowd shouted taunts and some pushed against the uniformed men guarding the woman on the post office steps.

Nessa took Daniel's hand and walked out into the street, trying to get closer. The woman continued reading, her voice gaining momentum over the crowd.

"We declare the right of the people of Ireland to the ownership of Ireland, and to the unfettered control of Irish destinies."

Nessa picked up Daniel and put him on her shoulders.

"The long usurpation of that right by a foreign people and government has not extinguished the right, nor can it ever be extinguished except by the destruction of the Irish people."

George appeared beside Nessa, smoking a cigar.

"In every generation the Irish people have asserted their right to national freedom and sovereignty; six times during the past three hundred years they have asserted it in arms. Standing on that fundamental right and again asserting it in arms in the face of the world, we hereby proclaim the Irish Republic as a Sovereign Independent State."

Mostly taunts and shouts came from the crowd.

"It's the proclamation of the provisional government," said George.

"I don't disagree in the least," said Nessa. "But it looks like most people just want their mail." Some in the crowd tried pushing against the men who formed a phalanx around the speaker on the steps. The speaker continued.

"The Republic guarantees religious and civil liberty, equal rights and equal opportunities of all its citizens, and declares its resolve to pursue the happiness and prosperity of the whole nation and of all its parts…"

Nessa watched a flag being hoisted above the massive grey

building. The words *Irish Republic* were sewn in gold over a green background. The crowd settled somewhat.

"...cherishing all the children of the nation equally, and oblivious of the differences carefully fostered by an alien government, which have divided us."

A second flag was hoisted on a different section of the roof. It was green, yellow and white.

"That's unity for ya," George said, puffing on the cigar.

"In this supreme hour the Irish nation must, by its valor and discipline and by the readiness of its children to sacrifice themselves for the common good, prove itself worthy of the august destiny to which it is called."

The woman rolled up the scroll and walked back into the post office, followed by the uniformed men.

"I can't decide which flag to salute," said George, as two flags were hoisted on different parts of the post office roof.

"I prefer the gold lettering on green, aesthetically," said Nessa. "But what a show!"

The three started walking northeast toward home in Drumcondra.

"She talked about children sacrificing themselves for the common good," said George. "I'm not sure I like the sound of that."

Gunshots rang out from the direction they'd come. Nessa instinctively ducked.

"Or that."

Nessa took Daniel's hand and they quickened their pace. As they arrived home, the gunfire had grown almost constant, and was punctuated with the explosive bark of grenades. Nessa had never heard the sound of a grenade. In the kitchen, George made tea, while Daniel sat on his mother's lap, burying his face in her breast.

"There's a lot of angry, young men out there with guns and bullets they didn't have yesterday," said George. "Believe me,

Nessa, I spend enough time at Reilly's to know they're lookin' to make an ugly mark on a world that won't have 'em."

*   *   *

4 a.m. Shelbourne Hotel, St. Stephen's Green, April 25, 1916

It was before dawn, and most of the men were asleep at the rebel encampment on Stephen's Green, near the center of Dublin. Amid the statues and fountains, fresh trenches scarred the spring grass.

At the east end of the public park stood the majestic Shelbourne Hotel, where British troops were quietly assembling machine gun nests in the fourth floor rooms facing the park.

At the first hint of ambient light, they opened fire onto the encampment fifty feet below. A hail of bullets ripped through tents and thudded into the turf. Rebels ran for the trenches or the closest copse of trees. They returned fire on the Shelbourne, but were withered by the relentless strafing of the machine guns fron above. Incendiary bullets set fire to the tents. The rebels retreated across the street to the Royal College of Surgeons.

Later that morning, General William Lowe arrived to take charge of the British forces. He sat in a luxurious, silver-studded chair in the Shelbourne Hotel ballroom, removed his gloves and lit a cigar.

"Where shall we place the eighteen-pounder? Bring me a street map! We are going to pulverize Liberty Hall!"

After placing the eighteen-pounder in reach of the heavily fortified newspaper office/munitions factory, General Lowe fired rounds of artillery for hours until Liberty Hall collapsed and burned.

When no one ran from the blaze, General Lowe began to suspect the embarrassing truth: The Citizen Army had abandoned the building the night before, leaving only the appearance that it was manned and fortified, with the express goal of wasting as many British bombs as possible.

*   *   *

1 p.m. Drumcondra, Dublin, April 26, 1916

"Da? Is that you, Da?" In her kitchen on Fitzgibbon Street, Nessa gripped the phone tight.

"Yes. Are you and Daniel all right?" The voice was faint.

"We're fine. I can't hear you very well. Where are you?"

"College of Surgeons." Gerald's voice became clearer. *"I'm helping the wounded from Stephen's Green. I don't know how long the phones will last. It's a battlefield..."*

Daniel came out of his room.

"Da?" The line crackled.

"Da?" Nessa heard a deep breath over the phone.

"I saw something today...now I wonder if it really happened."

"Tell me."

Nessa motioned Daniel onto her lap.

"It was just after eleven o'clock in the mornin' and we were in the middle of a firefight. Bullets were hitting the building, taking chunks of plaster down and breaking windows. The firing on our side was deafening. Right in the middle of all that, that's when the caretaker of Stephens' Green came out of his lodge, cool as you like, and started walkin' to the duck pond as if it were any other day. And the firing stopped. Not all at once, but by the time he got near the duck pond, the day was quiet as any other Wednesday. He broke the bread and threw hunks of it on the water, and the ducks swam toward him from every direction."

It was quiet for a moment. The line crackled. Nessa heard her father take a deep breath.

"This went on just long enough for everyone to wonder why the hell we were trying to kill each other. And for a few minutes after the caretaker went back in his lodge, it remained quiet. Then it all started up again."

"That's a beautiful moment, Da."

Nessa gently stroked Daniel's hair.

"It reminds of the bards who broke up a fight between the Fennians and the Gauls. They sang their hymns and their good poems to silence and to soften them. It was then they ceased from their slaughtering, on hearing the music of the bards, and they let their weapons fall to earth....'

"No bards today," said Gerald.

"The machine guns have been going since this morning, and the explosions—it feels like the end of the world." Her eyes welled up. "The end of the world I knew."

"I feel the same. But there's some brave lads out there, too. Rather than diving for cover when the Brits used hand grenades at Usher's Island, our boys grabbed 'em up and threw 'em back. Imagine? That was the last grenade those Limeys threw." Gerald laughed. Nessa smiled.

"Will you come stay with us when you need a break, Da?"

"Sure 'nough. With Ma gone, there's no one at home, anyway."

"Look after yourself, Da."

"Thanks dear. Pass me to Daniel."

Nessa held the phone to Daniel's ear.

"Be a good boy and do everything your Ma says."

"All right, Poppy."

After Daniel was asleep, Nessa poured herself a glass of red wine and looked out the window toward the downtown. She counted a dozen fires, some bigger than others. She took one of the shiny black disks from its brown paper sleeve, placed it on the

129

phonograph and set the needle. She cranked the handle in the side of the box to wind up the device.

Nessa loved the strange crackling sound before the song began, like the opening of a doorway to another world. She sat with her glass by the window and looked out at the flickering city. Fires were burning and she could hear the popping sound of faraway gunshots. The song played.

The pale moon was rising above the green mountain,
The sun was declining beneath the blue sea,
When I strayed with my love to the pure crystal fountain,
That stands in the beautiful Vale of Tralee.
She was lovely and fair as the rose of the summer,
Yet 'twas not her beauty alone that won me;
Oh no, 'twas the truth in her eyes ever dawning,
That made me love Mary, the Rose of Tralee.

Nessa stared out at the flickering fires. Tears rolled down her cheeks.

*   *   *

9 a.m. Tara Street, Dublin, Monday May 1, 1916

The center of Dublin was unrecognizable. Nothing was in its normal place. Hundreds of buildings had collapsed, Cars and trams were smashed and burned. The streets were littered with twisted metal, chunks of concrete, and broken glass. Acrid smoke from smoldering fires mixed with the smell of death and sewage. Nessa looked away from the bloating horses and human body parts as she and Gerald arrived at Tara Street.

Despite the carnage, thousands of Dubliners were out, quietly wandering the streets, staring at the shattered remains of a city they thought they knew. It was a shocking, awful sight. Here was the veil of civilization lifted.

All that remained of the bookshop was a pile of rubble. There was a slightly higher pile of rubble where the back office used to be, and they picked their way carefully through the wreckage towards it. Nessa's foot sank into a muddy hole, and she felt something sharp prick the bottom of her foot. Gerald took her arm as she pulled her foot from the mud. They cleared away pile of wood and plaster that covered an old safe.

"Thank goodness," she said, turning the dial. From inside she took a wood box with a cobra carved on top. She held the box closely as they made their way back to the street.

Chapter Twenty-five

Road from Cork to Castletownbere, May 1, 2009

I was taking it slow on the narrow road just south of Bantry Bay, heading to Castletownbere. Eight-foot high hedges lined the road for long stretches, creating a tunnel effect. T was tapping on his phone.

"When we get to town, you're going to notice something different about it," I said. "It might take you a few minutes, or an hour, but you'll notice it."

"You're not gonna tell me?"

"Nobody, not a single person, young or old, has a cell phone in their hand in public. Just warnin' you. I love it."

T put the phone away.

"What did you think of Brú na Bóinne?" I asked.

He pondered for a moment, looking out the windshield.

"I don't get why they call it a passage tomb. I mean, a tomb is where you bury people, and there's no one buried there. They said, maybe there was a ritual where they put bones in the basin. I don't know, that seems weird, like, why would you put bones in a basin."

We emerged from a tunnel of hedges.

"They're just guessing," I said, slowing for a tight curve around a massive outcrop of granite. "They don't even know who built it. When the Celts found it a couple thousand years ago, they made up their own stories about it, but they didn't know who built it, either. You're right, though, it's silly to call it a tomb when it wasn't built to bury people."

The sun flashed off a pond ahead.

"Yeah."

My eyes were readjusting from the flash when a small truck came around a corner, and I jerked the wheel right. The car skidded off the road onto dirt and gravel. I turned into the skid, but the back end slid left and we were spinning. I was helpless. Time stopped.

This can't happen. T's in the car.

I saw T's head move toward the windshield.

God don't hurt him.

Then everything was upside down.

*   *   *

The walls were painted blue with puffy clouds, and the blue pillar next to my bed was painted with orange and yellow flowers. I could see a sign on the wall. *What does it say?* The wall swam away.

There was a woman sitting and typing in a pink uniform. *She's at the nurse's station.* A few feet away from her, someone stood facing me, standing perfectly still. His pants, shirt, socks, shoes and gloves were white. *Is it a man?* I looked closer at his face. The skin was pale and scaly and his eyes…he disappeared. Gone. *They don't want me to see their eyes.*

I could see four or five of them, about ten paces apart from each other, standing still, facing me. Their arms were at their sides. When I looked too closely at their faces, they went away. *The ones*

133

who go away come back somewhere else, where I can't see them yet. Then the room went away.

I hear myself saying words. It sounds like the beginning of someone telling a story. I'm a large man with long hair to the middle of my back, wearing fine leather and furs, standing in the prow of a long wooden boat that's moving swiftly through the water. *The smell of sweat gives me strength. The scent of my queen gives me purpose.* A tall, beautiful woman, wearing white feathers in her long, brown hair, stands next to me. She studies the clouds.

The rhythm of the oars beats like a heart, splitting the waves into foam. The wide river gives way. At the site of a stone tower, we come ashore and the company gathers around it. I tilt my head back and bellow.

"Priest! It is a fine morning. Why do you hide? Where is your God?" My loud voice carries in the crisp air. I order my men to fell a tall oak. The rest dig a ramp down to the foundation of the tower. "Priest! How deep is your foundation? How firm is your faith? I will take it from beneath you!" The men hew the oak and dig the ramp.

"Priest! I am told your people have just one life. One life! What book can be written from just one life?" The words rang across the river valley. "But I have no more wish to see it ended than I would a whelp. Come down! You hide like a child!" The tall woman steps toward me.

"Are we felling the tower?"

"Not if he appears to me." The battering ram is almost ready, and a dirt ramp leads down to the foundation stones.

"And if he comes out?"

"I will give him a chance to speak."

"Good. I am curious to hear him describe their god. I would like to hear it this time."

CRACK! The men run the battering ram against the foundation of the tower. They swung it backwards and forward again. CRACK!

"Priest! Do you wish to be crushed among the falling stones? I have seen it! It is a bloody sight! But you may choose! My queen wishes to greet you, and speak about your god." It is silent for a moment. I nod and the men drive the oak into the base of the tower. CRACK! They dislodged a stone.

"Priest! I have seen many houses stronger than this. I have been a fish, a fox, an eagle! I keep course through storm-dark seas. I was champion of many skills at the Games of Tailtenn." I nod and the men drive the oak into the base of the tower. CRACK!

A middle-aged man appears at the open door of the tower. He holds books under his arm.

"Priest! You emerge."

"I heard a knocking. Who is here?"

I laugh.

"John. Checkin' vitals, John." I turned my head. A nurse in a baggy purple smock was holding my arm. "Open up."

"Mmm." I tasted the metal of the thermometer. The nurse examined the results

"Good."

"Still here?" I whispered.

"Doin' fine. Back to sleep."

The room darkened, my eyelids fell. The round tower came back. The priest is outside. My tall, beautiful consort walks around him slowly, then stops and addresses him.

"Your hair, your glory of manhood, is shaven away, your eyes are heavy with study, your flesh wasted with self-torture; your face is sad. I understand there are no women among you, no cheerful music, no laughter."

"We choose our way."

She walks up close to the priest, and takes his books away.

"Latin," she said. She opens the book and spits in the pages.

"How does a man make the world?"

"God said let there be light and there was light."

"And then he made the sun, the moon, and the stars."

"Yes."

"And the water. Did he make the water?"

The priest pauses. "He moved the water."

"But he did not make it."

"No."

"Who then?"

"There are great mysteries beyond—"

"Water is the great mother." She turns and walks away. "You deny her. You flog the flesh. You do not laugh, or suckle." She turns back to the priest. "What sickness is this?"

"Your ignorance—"

"QUIET!" I tower over him. "No cleric, not ignorance. The music we play fills our eyes with light. We listen for the song of the blackbird, the sound of wind and thunder, the cry of hounds let loose, the murmur of streams. We intercourse with women to the rhythm of the tiompan and strains of the harp." My anger is receding. My consort smiles. The priest speaks.

"O thou silly man, of whom I can get no good, if thou dost not cease praising the Fians, those pleasures that are in heaven thou shalt never enjoy."

I put my right hand on the handle of my sheathed sword, and looked closely into the priest's eyes.

"Tell me, will the King of Grace direct his servants to expel my hound from heaven?"

"The Lord will not suffer thee to bring a quadruped into heaven."

"My loyal hound, left behind?"

The priest shakes his head. I signal the company again. The oak ram crashes into the deepest foundation stones. Again, and again. A second stone dislodges. The tower groans.

"You would leave my hound behind? No, pale cleric. We will fell your tower and throw your books in the sea."

"You will share the after-life with the shrieking demons of hell, if you show no sign of repentance, my son."

I walk up to him. I smell roses. "In my time of death and burning I will rise in the smoke and fly in the clouds to the far horizon, to the turning fortress of northern stars, to joy and rest in timeless Tir na n Og."

"Nonsense—"

"Enough!"

I swing the sword over my left shoulder, landing the edge squarely on his bald skull, crushing the bone and splashing the brain. He falls in a heap. I look at the body.

"I grant your pitiful wish to live only once." Blood seeps onto the ground. I turn to the company. "Do not burn him. Put him in the forest where he will be scattered."

*   *   *

A doctor walked by then another nurse behind him. Standing against the wall opposite me was one of the people dressed in white, not moving. Its pale face was scaly like a fish, and the eyes bulged out like goggles. He disappeared when I looked too close. *They don't want me to see their eyes.* There were still four of them in the room, about ten paces apart. I stopped trying to look at them. I wondered what they were doing.

Waiting. The word came without thinking.

For what?

For you to stop breathing.

I'm not gonna stop breathing.

You're not breathing right now.

I took a sudden breath.

Open your eyes.

I opened my eyes.

Eat. It will make the fish-eyed people go away.

I asked for a turkey sandwich from a man wheeling equipment, and a nurse came over. She called for the doctor. I remember biting into the turkey and tomato and chewing it,

137

swallowing. I looked around for the standing people. I saw the
nurses coming and going. They were gone. That's when I
remembered to ask about T.

A few minutes later, a middle-aged nurse with long silver-
grey hair came in. I smelled lilacs. T walked in after her, his arm in
a sling and a bruise on his head. That moment in the car came
back, his head going forward, toward the windshield.

"Your head."

"Just a bump, the shoulder belt dislocated my shoulder. They
gave me a shot. It's OK now."

"You didn't smash your head."

"Not even a concussion," said the nurse. "The belt saved
him."

I took a breath.

"Good." I looked at T. He was looking at my legs. There was
a cast on the left one. I heard myself saying, "What happened?"

The nurse put her hand on my shoulder. I smelled the lilacs. T
looked pale, standing behind the nurse.

"You'll be good as new," she said. I looked at her. The silver-
grey hair framed a kind face with green eyes. "No need to worry,
love, we'll chase the pain away as best we can."

I nodded. She set up another morphine drip and left the room.

"What happened?" I asked T. He pulled a chair up to the bed.

"I don't remember much. Just skidding, flipping and going in
the water."

"What water?"

"The car went in a creek. You were…" His voice trailed off.

"What?"

"Drowned. Bloody. Not breathing." His eyes welled. "They
got you back."

"Not breathing? You mean dead?"

"They said for only a few minutes. That you were lucky."

"Dead."

I looked at the ceiling.

"Yeah."

"Wow."

I looked at T, and tried to smile.

"Yeah," said T. "Wow."

"Well, that explains a lot."

T looked at me sideways.

"Can you get me another sandwich?"

I told him about the big Viking, but left out the part about splitting the priest's skull. T said he'd been staying with Fio, Brian and the two kids. The nurse had called Fio to tell her I was awake. They were on their way. Suddenly I was tired. My whole body was tired. T sat in a chair while I dozed off.

*   *   *

The tall, beautiful woman is speaking to me.

"You do what your father and your grandfather did, what your brothers do."

"I live the way they live."

"Do you wish to make a mark?"

"I do."

"Then you must change the course of your family, as a great stone is set in a river, and the water flows around it. There is a river of hot blood flowing through this land that you must bend to the sea. If you bend this river of blood, it will wash into the sea, and we may live here in every season." My heartbeat grew faster. She smelled like spring. I listened close. "If the Christians believe they live just once, what does it matter? Let them believe what they will. If we live among them, they will shed their beliefs, and learn again the mastery of water and the cycle of lives…" I smile at her. She smiles back.

"Good morning!" I woke up. It was a new nurse. After a blur of words I was rolling in a hallway. The nurse's face was upside

139

down, blowing hair out of her mouth. The wheels squeaked, and the sound of voices grew. I rolled into my new room.

"Hey! I'm Lenny! I been 'ere since Mondee!" Lenny was an elderly man in a wheelchair with the kind of large, round stomach you could rest your arms on, and two metal peg-legs below his knees. His wheelchair was pointed at the TV, which was turned all the way up. Lenny was deaf in one ear and on powerful painkillers.

"Hi, I wish to bend a river to the sea."

It still sounded like someone else was talking.

"I'm gettin' out Saturdee!" Lenny enthusiastically licked his lips. "Out on Saturdee!" My cot rolled past the dividing curtain and into my share of the room. A family argument blared from the reality show on Lenny's TV.

"I won't put up with this anymore!" a woman's voice shrieked. "Don't you spin out of this driveway. Don't you SPIN OUT OF THIS DRIVEWAY!" (Sound of a muscle car burning pavement.) "That's IT! We're DONE!"

The nurse was turning down the bed. "Do you have earplugs?"

"I think so."

Relief washed over me. She came back in a minute with earplugs. I squeezed them in tight. If the volume was at ten before, now it was at nine.

"Do you have any other earplugs?"

"They come in different colors."

"Is there anything we can do about the TV?"

"Lenny'll be asleep before long."

As she turned to go, I felt something let go in my bowels.

"I could use a hand before you go." She came back to the bed. "The bathroom. It's been five days."

"Wow."

She helped me keep my balance on the way to the toilet. "Thank God my shift's over." I laughed.

What came next, over a period of about ten minutes, was the most gigantic and colossal pile that had ever emerged from my body in one sitting. There was little effort involved. The time had come. I couldn't help admiring it for a moment. For the first time in a week, *something* had gone right.

I felt a flush of pride as I walked past Lenny, who was nodding off. I found his clicker, slowly turned down the volume and made my way back to bed.

"Thank you," I whispered.

*   *   *

T was reading in the overstuffed pink chair when I woke up.

"Hey, man," said the morphine. He got up and came over.

"You look better."

"I feel better. Go ahead and take a seat." I pushed myself up and sipped some orange juice. "Helluva vacation for you."

"Never been on an airplane before."

"That's funny."

"Brian's getting me to Dublin for the flight tomorrow." He slung off his knapsack. "I brought the box back, with the letters. I was gonna read one for you if you want."

"Thanks, T, that's nice of you. I always figured reading to you in second grade would pay off one day." T laughed, but I knew he'd be shy about reading. "Maybe another time, when I'm not so looped on morphine."

"Got you a corned beef sandwich and a pickle." He put a paper bag on the table.

"You the man," I said, reaching out for a bro handshake. "Let's Skype when you get home. Don't tell your mother anything. Omerta."

"Sure."

When he'd left, I reached for the box and looked through the envelopes. There was one letter left I hadn't read, then the diary.

141

People of the Flow

Dearest Rigby,   April 14, 1916

I enjoyed receiving your blue envelope and the letter inside. I can hear your voice in the words, and it brightens the rest of the day. The bookshop has been quiet—we're steady on the bottom line with textbooks, and expecting a busy Christmas.

Daniel is putting sentences together. I can see his mind working from the expression on his face. His eyes light up when he masters a task, like tying his shoes or drying the dishes front and back. He continues to enjoy greeting the customers from behind the counter.

I've been harvesting your shelves for research into solstice temples, and sent Edward a letter to jog his memory. I came across a salacious bit of folklore in which a husband chases his naked wife around a dolmen under a full moon before sexual relations to improve their chances of having a child. This delightful past-time might never have been known to us today except that the Medieval Church expressly forbade both the practice of chasing the naked wife, and the emission of semen at ancient sites!

.More to the point, a new book that Edward ordered contained sketches of the Cairn at Davrinis, on the coast of Brittany. Its passage is also aligned to receive the winter solstice sun. Its dimensions make it about half the diameter of Brú na Bóinne, and it has a flat ceiling in the central chamber. There is little certainty as to its age, but the lack of a corbelled dome suggests it is older than Brú na Bóinne. Reading further brought about the discovery of the week: The nearest town is Carnac.

Your tome on etymology derives Carnac from cairn, and it's said that at night, little creatures called Morrigans dance around the mound in white clothes. I could find nothing on the etymology of Karnak in ancient Egypt. Perhaps Gamal knows.

142

Yesterday afternoon the anthropologist Charles Evans-Wentz came by and bought a dozen books. As I totaled the purchase, he spoke about his research into the commonplace occurrence of intermarriage in the ancient world.

After he left, I remembered references in O'Grady and Hyde to some of the great Celtic heroes being dark in complexion. It took me an hour, but I found the reference. O'Grady wrote that Diarmid Donn, a knight of the Fianna Eireen, was dark-haired and dark-complexioned. He was known as "the Brown," and was a great friend of Finn mac Cool. Hyde wrote that Ogma, the Tuatha Dé Danann given credit for inventing Ogham, was "brown…a Charon or Japetus." If people from the Near East or North Africa came this far north, perhaps it was they who built Brú na Bóinne.

Mother has been ill, and in the last few days has grown worse. Da thought it was a flu, but found red bumps on her belly this morning. They are at hospital while I wait for him to phone. I don't know what to tell Daniel. I look forward to another blue envelope—your last letter sounded so much like your voice. It was comforting. More and more, I think of us in New York.

For now, I will bring the story as far as it's come along in my mind, beginning with the Tuatha Dé Danann having discovered the whooper swan's mysterious winter home.

*   *   *

Danu led the way to the summit of the hill above the river, where the land spread out into a wide, flattened area, where they started making a camp. At the center of the summit, Danu came upon a thin slab of granite. Kneeling on the ground, she saw it was squared by hand. She whistled a short trill.

The company gathered quietly in the predawn darkness as Danu turned up the stone, to discover below a deep echoing space. It was not a cave.

143

She held a torch as they lowered her down by rope. The walls of the round room were stacked with stone slabs, each one reaching further to the center than the one below, steadily forming a dome to the height of three men.

In the round chamber, Danu ran her fingers over the smooth bowl of a large granite basin standing opposite from a passageway out of the room. Four others came down the rope with torches. The flickering light revealed spiral etchings and wavy lines on the massive stones. Danu led the others down the passageway, which was held up by tall granite pillars on each side.

The low passage made a slight turn and brightened. One by one, they emerged into daylight in front of a shallow pool—a granite boulder sat in the middle, deeply etched in spirals and reflected in the blue water.

The dawning sun sparkled on the quartz façade of the round temple, glowing brightest on a spot just a few feet to the right of the entrance. Further to the right, a large section of the quartz wall had collapsed and tumbled forward into the grass.

The sound of whoopers came from high above. "Whoop-ah, whoop-ah." A dozen swans came into sight, arriving from the northeast. They slowly circled three or four times, descending gracefully to join the flock across the river.

The Icelanders set camp on top of the mound, overlooking the swans' nesting area on the far side of the river. They played music, ate, and talked around a fire. They agreed that within a week the rising sun would reach the entrance and shine down the corridor and into the chamber, where the basin stood. They agreed to wait.

During the day they hunted stag, caught salmon and eventually befriended the tall, white wolves by leaving them shares of the meat. At sunset they gathered on the hill and listened to the music of the swans, sometimes playing along. Wondering and waiting. Over the next two mornings, the dawning rays of the sun sparkled on the white quartz face of the mound, coming closer to the entrance. The next night they sang a new song about the temple they had discovered in the winter home of the swans.

There is a womb of rock in the winter home.
and a basin of water inside it.
On the longest night's journey,
The dying sun awakens,
And first light shines,
stirring the waters of the basin.

As the song ended, there came a shouting hail. A man and a woman were climbing the mound. Their skin and hair were black. They were short in stature but thickly muscled. He wore his hair in thick cords, hanging beyond his shoulders and decorated with swan feathers. His right eye was chestnut brown. His left eye had been lost, and was replaced with an orbit of polished quartz. He carried a staff, but stood up ramrod straight, and seemed to have no need of it. Around his shoulder were three pipes attached to a large bag made of sheepskin.

The woman also kept her hair in long, thick cords, decorated with swan feathers. She carried a triple drum made from the trunk and two branches of a sycamore, covered in hide. She pointed to her heart, and said, "Boann." The man gave his name as Ogma.

Danu gave her name, as did the others in the company; the poet and musician Eochaid Ollathair, the smith Goibhniu, the physician Dian Cécht, the navigator Manannan mac Lir, Lugh of the Long Spear, the shapeshifter Oengus and the musical Caer Iborméith.

Ogma spoke and gestured, expressing that their people built the mound a thousand years before, but were afflicted with sickness that caused them long ago to return from where they came. He pointed southwest.

In a similar manner, Danu related to Boann and Ogma that they had sailed from the northwest, following the swans across the ocean to discover their winter home.

Ogma smiled and made clear his admiration for the boats he had seen tied off by the river. Then he blew into one of the pipes until the bag was inflated, and pressed back down on sheepskin. A pair of lingering notes hung in the air as Ogma put his fingers to the pipes, then the sound fled up an octave and down again. The swans in the pool swam closer and trilled. Danu and her company picked up their branch-bells, timpan and harp.

Soon enough, the harmonies of the pipes and harp together flowed around the heart of Boann's beating triple-drum, the swans called and bugled in the steam, and the music carried in the cold night.

*　　　　　*　　　　　*

Rigby, you are always on my mind, making your rounds in the land of the sun. It can't be too soon for you to come back to the land of clouds.

All of my love,
Nessa

Chapter Twenty-six

Townland of Disert, County Cork, Ireland, May 5, 2009

In the hospital I couldn't feel my left wrist or left ankle, but when I woke up at home from the throbbing, I got out my pills and took two. Then I poured the rest in the sink to count them. One went down the drain before I closed the stopper. Good thinking.

There were sixty. I couldn't remember if I could get more. Taking two pills at a time would cover the pain from two walks a day for fifteen days. The pills took the pain from an "eight" to a "three," or the difference between being unable to think straight and having a mildly pleasurable day.

I had a blue walking boot on my left ankle, a green cast on my left wrist and a brown recliner on the screened-in front porch. The recliner was set up for me with tables on either side of the lazy boy to manage the laptop, headphones, beverage and fan. The big Viking in my head loved the fan. He was drawn to it immediately. *Spinning blades! Are there other things like this?* The music really threw him. I explained what was going to happen, that he was about to hear music coming out of the little boxes, but nothing prepared him for Led Zeppelin. I played *Kashmir*, and he loved it, and wanted to hear more, so I played all their albums for the first

time in years. *My brothers.* He asked for liquor, but settled for
Guinness. *A stout drink.*

So drinking a pint of Guinness in front of an old oscillating
fan after an afternoon walk on a hot July day on the front porch of
the home I grew up in was not so bad. The Guinness would extend
the pills. The pain was manageable. The problem was sleeping. A
jangling ball of free-floating anxiety had come home with me from
Cork City. In every moment it felt like there was a catastrophe
waiting. When I told Fiona I was getting a raggedy two or three
hours a night, she promised to stop by with a bag of Indica.

For my old normal self, anxiety was a warning that pointed to
a problem, which I could either fix or not fix. It was a red flag that
came and went. After the accident, it just stayed. Looming. It was
there with my toast and butter in the morning, and it came along on
my morning walk. By late afternoon, my jaw was tight, one or both
of my legs were twitching and I tasted metal.

As the sun fell below the trees, I saw Fiona drive up and park.
Hallelujah. She walked to the porch with a couple of grocery bags.
I got up and followed her into the kitchen with my crutches.

"How far d'ya get today?" she asked.

"To the cove."

"You look like shite. Sort of grey."

"Thanks."

"I brought your meds." She put a zip-lock bag on the table.
"It's the kind that makes you sleepy, the Indica. It's blueberry
something. There's a little glass pipe in there, and some papers."
She took a small stack of DVDs from her gigantic bag. "I found
some Scooby Doo that wasn't covered in peanut butter, and some
others."

"Why, thank you very much indeed. Scooby's the best.
Except for Bugs."

I got busy trying to roll a joint, while Fiona sat on the top step
with a cigarette.

"How're ya keepin'?"

"Well," I paused, rolling the joint between my thumbs and middle fingers. *Like riding a bike*. "There's a Viking in my head that caved some priest's head in with a big sword, but all in all, he seems a good fella. He's very much into Zeppelin right now, and Aerosmith, and Rory Gallagher."

"Still on the morphine?"

"You betcha." I licked the paper and twisted it home.

"And there's just the one?"

"One what?" I lit the joint.

"One Viking in your head."

"Yeah, well, no—there's a tall, elegant woman, who says very sensible things, like I should stop whackin' priests on the head, and that I should bend the river of blood to the sea."

"Well that *is* sensible."

"Yeah." I was feeling a mental warmth that was very pleasant. "Of course, there's the big boat and my company of men."

"Of course." Fio took a drag of her Gitanes, and let it out slowly. "So, given the number of people knockin' around in there, though no more than usual I don't wonder, what's a day in the life like out here?"

I offered the joint but she declined.

"Wake up, wash up, toast and jam with morphine, then a walk, as long as I can manage. Then I come home and peel two oranges and a grapefruit, blend 'em up with ice, and have a cold drink in front of the fan. It's all repeated in the afternoon. After dinner, I might listen to music, read something or finish up the old letters. We've recently discovered the fizz in coke and that it goes beautifully with rum. He loves to burp."

"I can imagine. Good to see you're followin' doctors orders—"

"In the daytime I do, mostly."

"Anything more in the letters?" Fio stubbed out her cigarette.

"Nothing that explains what happened to them. But I'll tell you; our great-grandparents were a pretty romantic pair—like, really in love. They were both into dolmens and the Celts, and ancient temples, especially Brú na Bóinne..."

I took the last two letters out and handed the wood box to Fiona.

"You should see for yourself. Take 'em. I'll get you these last two when I'm done."

"Thanks." The box disappeared into her giant purse. "Hey, we're closing on the store in two weeks."

"Thanks for dealing with all that."

I got up from the chair and we hugged goodbye.

"No worries. We'll both get a check—Da's last present."

I sat back down. "Be nice to see the old place still goin'."

"I know," she said, walking down the steps. "Enjoy the medicine! And Scooby."

"Thanks!" I waved as she pulled away.

My laptop buzzed. T was Skyping. He waved at the camera.

"You got back ok. Thanks for calling."

"Yeah, it was cool. I sat next to a nun. What about you?"

"I'll be ok. I didn't lose any important parts, as far as I can tell, though I might have gained some. How's your Mom?"

"She's good."

"You didn't tell her."

"Naw, it would just make her upset for no reason. I'm fine."

"When does work start?"

"Tomorrow."

"Have you seen what's-her-name?"

"No, I haven't even thought about her."

"Then the trip was a success! You're over being dumped."

T laughed. "Yeah right."

"Say hi to your Mom for me, and be careful at work. Lift with your knees."

I settled into the recliner, thankful for the sweet-smelling bag of cannabis. After several tokes of self-medication, I opened the musty green-leather edition of *Cormac's Glossary* I'd found in the attic with Uncle Fran. It was a list of Gaelic words and their meanings, written in the fifteenth century, based on a manuscript called *The Speckled Book*, originally written for King Cormac mac Cuilleanain in the ninth century. I took a slug of rum and coke, and browsed through the As and Bs.

Basc means decorative beads made from jewels taken from a dragon's head when still alive.

A toast to that! I took another slug.

Biror meant a well or a stream, hair, hairs of a stream. *Buas* meant to have knowledge of the poetic art. *Buanann* was nurse of the heroes, a teacher of championship skills. I limped into the kitchen to refresh the drink.

In the Ds, I was surprised to find *Disert*, the townland in which I'd grown up and where I was presently recuperating, spelled *Disert*. I'd seen it as *Disert* and *Disart* in Parish records. In *Cormac's Glossary*, the entry said: *Though barren now, a great house was there before*. A note said *stripped* was an alternate meaning for *barren*.

I didn't know of any ancient ruins in Disert. Not even close. It was a handful of old farmhouses and stables, and a few modest retirement homes, recently built. It was a rocky hand reaching into the Atlantic, with steep hills, hidden coves and a few wide places you might call a pasture. On my morning walk, I would take Da's binoculars to see if I could spot something. For now, my brain could handle Scooby-Doo, but little else. I took another toke, held it as long as I could, and turned on the TV. Smiling, I soon fell asleep to *Adventures on Zombie Island*.

The next morning, having already walked further than the day before, I saw an old man through the binoculars. He was ahead of me on the path, looking out over a cove. A tall Irish wolfhound sat at his feet.

As I approached, the dog noticed me first and then the old man. His face was ruddy, acquired when living by the ocean, always in the wind. I walked up to them.

"Paddy Sullivan," he said. We shook hands. "This is Fergus." I patted his head.

"John Harrington."

"Are you Gerald's boy?" I nodded. "I was sorry to hear."

"Thanks." Paddy squeezed the dog's ruff, patted her head and started back on the track. "Do you mind if I tag along?"

"You look a bit banged up."

"They tell me I'm supposed to walk a little longer every day."

We walked in silence for a few minutes. Fergus ventured out a few yards in front of Paddy, but never far. I couldn't keep quiet for long. I was still a reporter. I always had questions.

"Are you retired?"

"I run sheep on t'other side of the hill."

We walked again in silence.

"What was it like growin' up here when you did?"

Paddy bent down, picked up a good-sized stick and threw it. Fergus took off in a flurry of rusty fur.

"I used to walk the hills on the weekends, like this. I wasn't into football. My aunt read to us every night, so I became a reader, anything I could find. There's a good library in Castletownbere, and a great one in Cork City."

"I've been meaning to go…" Fergus returned with the stick and placed it at Paddy's feet. "There ya go, girl." He squeezed her ruff, patted her head, picked up the stick, and threw it ahead. Fergus took off like a shot. We started walking again.

"Have you ever heard of an old monastery around here? Old ruins?"

"Old ruins are everywhere. You're walkin' next to one."

Fergus returned, sat down, and started chewing on the stick. Paddy kept walking. Fergus got up to follow, forgetting about the stick.

"What was school like?"

"The priests ran the schools. The national law was to keep religion and education separated, but then they handed the school system over to the priests."

"You're kidding."

"Not a bit. There I was, ten years old, bein' told I'm a sinner. Well, I said, feckin' hell, don't give me that bullshit."

"Did you ever say anything back?"

Paddy stopped. The dog stopped. He looked me in the eyes.

"One time I asked the priest why he wasn't livin' in poverty like Jeeeeesus."

"What'd he say?"

We started walking again. The trail descended toward a small cove.

"He didn't like it one bit. Any time I asked a question, the answer came back the same: It's a mystery, they said, you're not meant to understand it—but ya sure better believe it." Paddy sat on a boulder by the water. I did the same. "They never taught us about the Troubles. I was twenty-five years old when I learned about the strikes and the Easter Risin' from the TV. The priests never told us."

"Why?"

"I suppose they didn't want any troubles of their own." We sat quietly. "New Year's Eve, 1969. The pub 'ad just hooked up the TV antenna, and it was gettin' 'round midnight. When they turned on the set, there was the Beatles with their long hair, singin' *All You Need is Love*. We about fell off our stools. The priests hadn't mentioned them boys."

The Dilaudid was wearing off. I would be glad to see the recliner. We made our way back up the track. The setting sun was behind us.

"You mentioned ruins," said Paddy. "Closest thing'd be three standing stones past the north edge of the property. They're big. Haven't moved an inch in a few thousand years."

"D'ya think they were part of a ring once?" Paddy's thick brogue was inspiring the return of my accent.

"Could be."

At the spot where we met, we stopped to catch a breath. The pain was six and a half out of ten. Not too bad. Paddy patted Fergus' ruff as the dog sat at his feet.

"The priests called out the names of everyone and how much they gave on Sunday, I remember that," said Paddy. "Con Murphy never gave anything, and at the end of the list, the priest would say, 'Con Murphy—bugger all.' But Con didn't care; he was his own man."

"They called out people's names?"

"They did." Paddy snorted. "Y'know Father Walsh in town gets a new car every year. He thinks no one notices because it's the same color, but it's a new car every year, sure enough."

We shook hands and parted ways.

"I'll be walkin' out here at least another week," I said. "Hope to see you again."

"Always nice to have a bit o' company."

Chapter Twenty-seven

Townland of Disert, County Cork, May 6, 2009

*T*he *slender chains of gold and amber are poetry.*

The words were back in my head. I was on the front porch, reading from a stack of books that Nessa and Rigby must have read during their schooling. I was halfway through *A Literary History of Ireland: From Earliest Times to the Present Day*, by Douglas Hyde, published in 1903.

Hyde wrote of an etching or painting showing a Celtic scene, as described by the Roman writer Lucian.

"Ogmios was a very old man with a bald forehead, grey hair and a chain attaching his tongue to the ears of half-a-dozen men. The chain is made from slender cords of gold and amber, and the men are merry. They take up the chain's slack so they might not miss a word. The words of Ogmios were lances, sharp and swift to pierce the mind."

The chain is language.

The Viking's voice did not respond to what I thought, or what I said out loud. He responded to what came in front of my eyes, or in this case, to what I was reading. He always loved it when I turned on the fan. Every time, he stared at the turning blades.

I will never leave this thing of beautiful make.

He liked Rory Gallagher too. I had a DVD of a concert in Belfast in 1974, when it was really bad there, and he sang a song about comin' home that got the crowd jumpin' and wild. In the interviews, he was soft-spoken, a friendly man who died young.

The good people liked 'is playin' so much, they took him back.

Suddenly I was thinking about whiskey. A shot to Rory. I poured out the Dullamore Dew. Down it went.

Rory had a slender silver chain 'round the crowd, same as 'round the swans, when they sing and fly in the night.

I lit a cigarette and Googled swans and gold chains. Up came an old woodcut. The swans were linked together by thin chains, like Ogmios and the men who followed him, like Rory and the crowd.

Magic.

The words were a little swimmy, but I turned the page. I rubbed my eyes and poured another shot.

"During a lively feast, the Fennians and the Golls take arms against each other in a bloody battle that lasts for hours, with terrible slaughter and maiming, until the bards arrive at the hall and sing their hymns to calm and soften the hearts of the fierce combatants. It was only then that both sides let their weapons fall to earth, and the poets took up their weapons, and went between them, and grasped them with the grasp of reconciliation."

I listened to myself laugh.

Blood running with beer yes, but not slaughter. It was the heroic bards who wrote the verse, was it not? The same brave men who broke up this fearful night of maiming with their exceptional musicianship? More likely it was a lesser affair, waiting only to be spun into a hero's tale.

I drank the shot, lit a cigarette, and skipped over four pages of poems. The next page was titled: *Tales of Bru na Boinne.* Hyde wrote, "Aengus asks Dagda, his father, to borrow Bru na Boinne for a day and a night. When Dagda returns, Aengus says that because a day and a night at Bru na Boinne is the same as forever, he would keep possession."

I took a drag of the cigarette, feeling it mix with the whiskey in my throat, which chuckled.

There is no one in single possession of the Bru. The story is truth in a jest. In the black darkness of the chamber at Bru na Boinne, in the rhythmic music and echoes of verse, there is timelessness. This is known, and thus Aengus plays on the knowledge.

On the next few pages were more poems. The Viking read out the last three lines.

"A beautiful game, most delightful
Men and gentle women under a bush
Without sin, without crime."

I took a last drag and stubbed out the butt halfway through. The Viking sighed.

"Why do we remain on this porch?" he asked. *"Is there not a hall to drink in?*

I fell asleep in the chair.

Chapter Twenty-eight

Sanatorium at Peamount, Newcastle, County Dublin June 18 1916

Rigby and Gerald moved quietly in the shadows of a moonlit night, down the wide back steps of Peamount Sanitorium, with a stretcher between them. A grey blanket covered Nessa's body.

George Russell opened the back doors of a green British Army truck. Rigby and Gerald slid the stretcher inside and climbed in after it. George took the wheel and headed for the service gate. On the other side of the grounds, the staff had formed a bucket line with the fire brigade, putting out a fire that was burning a large gazebo at the center of the front gardens.

Rigby and Gerald moved Nessa onto a makeshift bed in the back of the truck. She groaned but didn't wake.

"You shouldn't have come back," said Gerald. "I really didn't think you would."

"Desert?"

"Yes, it's a capital crime."

"My world is in this truck." Gerald was quiet. "She's strong. We'll go to New York. There must be hundreds of Harringtons there. It'll be safe." The blanket stirred. Nessa opened her eyes.

"That voice…Rigby?" asked Nessa, in a weak voice.

"Yes it's me, I'm here." A smile spread on Rigby's face. He

158

smoothed her hair.

"Where are we going?"

"Home, to the Beara, so Aunt Clara can take care of you."

"Where is Daniel?"

"Already there."

Rigby poured water from a thermos into a tin cup and offered it to Nessa. She sat up and took a sip. Rigby put a damp facecloth on the back of her neck and smoothed her hair. She lay back down.

"I had a dream of Lady Gregory's garden," said Nessa. The wheels slid in the mud and the truck lurched sideways.

"I remember that day," said Rigby. "Doug Hyde recited the entire lineage from Queen Macha to Queen Nessa over tea and scones."

Nessa smiled at Rigby.

"With raspberry jam," she said.

"If I recall correctly, Nessa, the daughter of Echid Yellow-heel, agreed to marry Fachtna, the Giant King of Ulster, and bore him a son, Conor," said Rigby. "But for all his size and strength, one day King Fachtna passed to the next world, and it was voted that his step-brother Fergus succeed him."

George stirred, coughed and took a drink from his flask. The cart swayed. Rigby continued.

"Queen Nessa agreed to marry Fergus on condition that the youthful Conor be named king for a year, just to see how it would go. For that year as king, Conor was so wise and the land so prosperous that the people wanted him to stay, and Fergus was content to have it so, for what he wanted most of all was to please Queen Nessa, whom he had always secretly adored. So Fergus remained at young Conor's court for a time, and was honored by the people for his willingness to cede the power that could have been his."

Rigby paused for effect, and Nessa's weak voice broke the silence.

"Do you believe it's all true? Or a lot of fanciful stories, as old

Mr. Piggott would have us believe?"

"The bards were fond of garnishment and flourish of course," said George, "but inside the fancy wrappin' was the everlastin' truth. If ya' choose to hand your stories down by memory, they'd better be memorable. That doesn't make 'em false. That's what the English never understood, bein' so literal and all, present company excluded." George nodded at Rigby and took a drink from the flask.

"Please continue Rigby," said Nessa. Rigby cleared his voice.

"One mornin' under Conor's reign, round about a hundred and fifty B.C., a flock of birds descended on the fruit trees at Emain Macha, bringin' Conor, Fergus an' all the king's men out with their slings and a flurry of stones, and the birds flew off to a field of barley, and the men followed again with their slings. Over and over, the birds lure the men across the countryside until they found themselves at Brú na Bóinne, the great mound of the ancients. In a nearby hut Conor and Fergus discovered a male infant, abandoned, and took it back to Emain Macha, where he was mentored by Aife and Scathach, and grew up to become the hero Cuchulain."

"The birds heard the crying child," said Nessa.

"I suppose so yes," said Rigby. "And they went to get people to come take care of it."

"And the birds kept drawing the men to the hut even when they were being pelted by stones."

"Yes," said Rigby.

"Thank you for the wonderful story. I think I'll sleep now." She nestled across Rigby's chest. He held her in his arms as her mind slipped into the past.

*   *   *

The driveway was long and straight in the shade of old oaks on either side of the road. Rigby had the reigns of the cart as they approached Lady Gregory's estate. The road crossed a wooden bridge over a wide ditch and suddenly they were inside a gigantic circle ringed with hedges. The clamshell driveway surrounded a central fountain that extended into an oval-shaped shallow pool, where a pair of geese were preening themselves. The wooden cart wheels crunched over the white shells.

"Good lord," whispered Nessa.

"Yes indeed," said Rigby, as they got out of the cart. The front door was open and they could hear music. The geese hopped out of the pool and waddled toward them.

"Would the lady like to go inside?" asked Rigby, bowing.

"Yes, thank you."

Lady Gregory appeared at the open door.

"Don't let those silly geese shake water all over you!" she bellowed. "They love to do that!" Lady Gregory took Nessa's arm and walked into the house, past a grand staircase and into a large room overlooking the gardens. Life-sized sculptures stood here and sat there. Landscape paintings of green valleys and billowing clouds hung on the walls. Half a dozen people sat in overstuffed couches and chairs forming a circle in the middle of the room, where an oval-shaped table of black marble was covered in plates of food, wine and bowls of fruit. Ornate standing lamps, hanging plants and an ornate standing birdcage completed the scene.

"This is Cybele," said Lady Gregory, gesturing to the parrot. "Cybele, this is Queen Nessa."

"RAAWWK. QUEEN NESSA!"

Lady Gregory laughed.

"Very good Cybele!" She gave the bird a small piece of bread. "She doesn't always get it right the first time. I think she likes you. I assume you know of Queen Nessa and King Fachna, Fergus and Conor."

"I do," said Nessa. "But I wonder if even Queen Nessa was ever announced by a parrot."

Lady Gregory laughed and lifted her glass. Someone put a record on the phonograph.

"Please join us," she said, ushering Rigby and Nessa onto an empty two-seater couch, completing the circle. The song played.

The pale moon was rising above the green mountain,
The sun was declining beneath the blue sea,
When I strayed with my love to the pure crystal fountain,
That stands in the beautiful Vale of Tralee...

"VALE OF TRALEE! RAAWWK!" Cybele screeched.
Returning from the phonograph, Douglas Hyde emerged from behind a statue and sat next to Lady Gregory on the couch opposite. With a smile and a magician's flourish, Hyde removed a packet from his leather satchel and placed it on the marble table.

"The translation is done, said Hyde. "And quite remarkable, though fragmented of course. I can only make an informed guess at the date, but from the style of verse I'd say it was Ossianic, somewhere in the middle of the eighth century."

Hyde handed Nessa a single piece of paper. Rigby peered over her shoulder.

"That is the sum total of what I could make out," said Hyde, tamping down the tobacco in his pipe. "As you can see, there were enough words in a row here and there to suggest one thing or another, so essentially one is left with a smidgeon of this and a smidgeon of that. I'd say Nessa that you should take it out for a drive in the light of modern times, and fill in the blanks whichever way you like..."

     *   *   *

Rigby held Nessa in his arms, her head cradled in his shoulder. He smoothed her orange hair. Gerald lifted Nessa's sanatorium tunic to check her abdomen. There were more rosy spots. Typhoid. The fever would either break, or she would die.

"The first time you came into my bookstore, it felt like someone had turned up the lights on a stage," Rigby said. "When you came to the counter and looked at me with kindness, my knees were jelly. It was all I could do to count change."

A carriage clattered past in the other direction.

"Our walks to the Yveaugh Gardens, and the Ha'Penny Bridge. My tongue was talking, somehow, while the rest of me was in a state of utter disbelief that I was there with such a woman."

Rigby kept talking, as if Nessa were awake, remembering the places they'd been and the people they met. Every so often Nessa groaned or coughed. She opened her eyes for a time, and Rigby thought at first she was awake, but she didn't speak. Gerald remembered the night when she was a small child, in the attic, staring at the storm. She had the same look. *Between this world and the other.*

In the first light before dawn, the wheels slid into a deep rut. The carriage swayed over to one side, and it seemed to hang in space before righting itself with a clatter. Suddenly, Nessa sat up, and looked around. "My notes." Rigby pulled the blanket back over her shoulders. "My primer, I must finish." Rigby took a notebook from her leather bag, and handed it to Nessa. She held it to her chest. Her eyes closed, and she slept in Rigby's arms.

The green truck was warming in the midday sun. Gerald had the wheel while George slept in the back. Rigby held Nessa. Her breathing was shallow but steady. The truck slowed to a stop as they approached a pond about twenty miles south of Bantry.

"We should get her out in the air, wash her as best we can," said Gerald. "The sun is warm."

As they moved Nessa onto the stretcher and covered her with towels, George woke up. Rigby and Gerald brought the stretcher down a single-track path to the shoreline, where purple and yellow flowers turned in the breeze. George made a fire for the kettle.

When the water was warm, Gerald soaped a cloth, dipped it in the kettle and cleaned Nessa's face and neck, as Rigby held her in his arms. She opened her eyes.

"Rigby." She smiled. "I smell the ocean."

"We're just south of Bantry, going home to Disert, so you can recover." Nessa looked at Rigby with a faint smile.

"Mmmm." With her arms around the notebook, she closed her eyes. Rigby took the cloth and continued washing.

"What is this cut on her foot?" he asked.

"It might be what started the infection," said Gerald.

"How did she cut it?"

"I'm not sure exactly, she didn't mention it."

After toweling Nessa dry, Rigby and Gerald walked the stretcher back up the path to the truck. Inside, Rigby set aside the heavy wool blanket and pulled a cotton one over Nessa. Her lips were bluish.

"Gerald!" he shouted. "Come here!"

Nessa's chest was still. Rigby pulled aside the blanket and pushed the clothing from her breast. He listened at her heart.

"What's wrong?" Gerald was at the back door. "Oh no." He jumped in the truck and felt her wrist for a pulse. He moved his fingers and felt again. He put his ear to her heart.

"She was talking," said Rigby. "She knew me."

At the door of truck, George removed his cap.

Gerald walked to the pond, kneeled down and splashed his face with water. He looked up to the sky, and spoke quietly.

"Rest in the wind, Nessa. If they don't let you in, I'll break down the door."

Chapter Twenty-nine

Castletownbere, County Cork, June 1, 2009

Young children burst out the door and down the steps of the Castletownbere Library as I approached. Inside the foyer was a bulletin board with an old wooden sign over it, hand-painted with the word, *Leabharlann,* At the children's table inside sat a somewhat dazed looking woman with long dark hair.

"I need coffee," she said to herself.

"They must be hard to keep up with." She looked up. Her hair was jet black and gathered in a ponytail. Her eyes were blue. Her skin was alabaster, whiter than ivory.

"I can't decide if they keep me young or make me old." She stood up from the children's table and held out her hand. "Keira. How can I help you?"

"John Harrington, from the States."

We shook hands and sat down at an adult-sized table by the front window, where she opened a brown leather book. There was no one else in the library. I was light-headed from cannabis, which was helping wean off the morphine. I forgot why I came. Keira flipped through the brown leather book. Her fingers were long and slender.

"When was this building built?"

She looked up.

"1851. There was a tobacconist here 'til the Gaelic League opened the library in 1900." There was a rushing sound in my head. I was glad to be sitting down. Patches of silvery color sparkled in my peripheral vision.

"I saw the old Gaelic sign in the foyer."

Keira's finger ran down a page and stopped. What was she doing?

"The original Gaelic surnames of the Harringtons were variations on Ingardail. The British officially changed them to Harrington in the late sixteenth century, but there's always been Gaelic nicknames attached to different branches of the family tree. There's a branch on Bearhaven Island with the name Caobach, meaning black-backed gull. Do you know what branch you are?"

She thinks I'm an American climbing up the family tree. I don't sound all that Irish after twenty years gone, not compared to the good people of Castletownbere. She must have people coming in all day asking about their family tree. That's why the big book is on the front table.

"British."

"Oh."

"I grew up outside of town, in Disert."

"Ah, you grew up here."

Speak slowly and clearly. The words should come out one by one.

"My great-grandfather was Rigby Harrington, born in England 'round 1885, and managed an antiquarian bookstore in Dublin by 1910, when he met Nessa Ó Dálaigh, a nice Irish girl from Disert, who was attending Dublin City College." I was hearing a little echo of everything I said. "They had a son, my grandfather Daniel, and they wrote letters back and forth while she kept the bookstore, and he was a supply officer in the British Service Corps in Egypt. He deserted in June 1916, and disappeared. Probably changed his name."

"How do you know they wrote letters?"

"I have them."

I took the old wood box from my knapsack. Keira's eyes grew wide. There was something feline about their shape. I opened the lid.

"May I?"

I nodded. She picked up the lock of hair, and held it up to mine. "Is this your great-grandmother's hair?"

"I believe so. She was an Ó Dálaigh. I didn't know I was one eighth English 'til I read the letters." My head felt bouncy. "Thought I was Irish head to toe." Keira smiled.

"There's not a family I know that tells the whole truth," she said.

"I'm finding that out, but I can't help trying to put together the bits and pieces. I want to know what happened to Rigby, and I can't find a death record for Nessa." It felt like part of me was saying the right words, and pulling the helpless parts of me along. I wasn't all on the same page. *Maybe that's why there's an echo.*

"The birth and death records are kept by the Parishes, and they're usually very thorough and accurate. How about their son? Your grandfather."

"Died before I was born. Early '60s. He's buried somewhere around here."

"Well John, it's a more interesting puzzle than usually walks through the door, I'll give you that. I took you for an American at first."

"I spent 20 years in the States—some of the accent wore off."

"Back now, are we?" My head was starting to feel somewhat more normal.

"Hard to say."

"Have you read the letters?"

"Yes, they're very romantic." I paused. The echo was gone. "They loved the Celtic legends, Brú na Bóinne and the Tuatha Dé

Danann. I can say that Nessa wasn't a big fan of the Catholic church."

"That's not a big surprise in that time. Irish women were starting to push back against things like churching."

"Churching?"

"There was a blessing required for women to be accepted back into the church after giving birth, which was considered unclean, that kind of thing."

Something fell into place in my head. "Maybe she didn't want a Christian burial." There was something in the first letter. I took it from the envelope and found what I was looking for on the first page.

"I saw a priest on the street last night who looked very much like Father Kerry from St. Mary's in Castletownbere. I remembered sitting in the pews as he barked about the devil abiding in our flesh, thrusting the donation-basket on its long stick under our noses, one by one, promising salvation in exchange for silver. It's a terrible injury to young minds to be shamed for sins they never committed, to begin the needless cycle of guilt and deliverance. I can't watch it happen to Daniel."

"Lovely writing," said Keira. "I don't disagree with her. Your great-grandparents grew up in the Celtic Revival. People were translating thousand-year-old Gaelic texts for the first time, rediscovering the pre-Christian legends, celebrating the music and verse of the ancient druidic poets. It must have been a wild time. Where did you find the letters?"

I told her about Da's death, and how Fran and I found the old wood box sitting on what must have been Nessa's rocking chair in the attic of the family house in Disert, along with an 1886 edition of *Cormac's Glossary* in green leather.

"How do you suppose the box got in the attic?" Keira said. "Who would do that?" *Why hadn't I thought about that?* "I know I wouldn't leave my own hair in a box—more likely it was her husband."

"Probably." *Jet black hair, blue feline eyes, and smart.* "It's the kind of thing you might do if you were never planning to come back. Like a memorial."

"But with the last name Harrington, he could have changed his first name and lived his life out on the Beara amidst hundreds of Irish Harringtons—almost the perfect place for him to disappear."

"True enough."

"At any rate, we'd love to have the letters on exhibit." I paused. "When you're ready."

"Yeah, sure. The library should have them."

"Hold on, let me get some gloves to handle them properly."

Keira disappeared into a back room and came back with two pairs of white cotton gloves. I handed her the letters. She examined the paper with a magnifying loop.

"The age is right," she said. "You were fortunate to find these, with your Da's passing. Something to hold on to." *Black hair, blue eyes, smart and thoughtful.*

"Would you have lunch with me?" There was something involuntary about the words coming out. "I passed Jack Patrick's Butcher down the street—the place with a poem on the window. And I really would like to learn more about the Celtic Revival."

"I'll go to lunch, if you'll read me the poem on the window."

Good. I was made to read poems to women. We gathered our things and she locked the library, leaving a note on the door, "Back after lunch."

A few minutes later, on the narrow Main Street sidewalk, I reached back for my once robust Irish accent and read the white-washed script.

"In a kitchen quite neat,
Full of good things to eat
With aromas of pickles and spices—"
An old man with a cap stopped on the sidewalk to listen.
"I hum as I'm baking,

Rolling sieving or grating.
I thumb recipe pages,
Handed down through the ages,
Using generous measures,
I make golden crust treasures.
Thank goodness for food from the heart."

Keira's smile changed her face, and the air around her. The old man tipped his cap and moved on. Inside, we ordered sandwiches and sat in a booth by the front window. I saw the butcher and his wife were both pleasantly plump. A good sign.

"So," said Keira, who had brought along a notebook. "Your great-grandfather deserted from Egypt in June 1916. Just after the Uprising in Dublin. He had a bookstore, presumably in the downtown."

"Tara Street."

She made a note.

"Could the Uprising have something to do with it?" I asked.

"Maybe. The British Navy shelled the sh...the living hell out of the downtown from the Liffey. Chances are good his store was bombed or burned at the hands of the British Navy, his own boys. Could be a reason to desert."

"Weren't deserters executed?" As the words came out of my mouth, it sounded like two people talking, or there was an echo.

"Very few were actually put to death," said Keira.

The plates arrived. My salivary glands responded immediately to the smell of corned beef and the sight of a root beer float. I almost drooled before taking a large bite of the sandwich, then half the pickle.

"Mmmmm." When bits of onion dropped in my lap, and I felt mustard on my chin, I suspected the Viking was enjoying the meal as much as I. *Take smaller bites.*

Keira ate methodically: one bite of grilled bass, one bite of beets, a forkful of brown rice and a sip of lemonade.

"Do you have brothers and sisters, uncles and aunts?"

I sucked out a third of the root beer float. The Viking got a kick out of the straw. It had one of those bendy tops.

"My sister Fio is in Cork City with her husband Brian and two twin boys, and I've an Uncle Fran in town. He's been in the merchant marine all 'is life. Out on a job now. Back in a week or so." I demolished a healthy chunk of the sandwich. "Mmm." I took the plastic top off the root beer float to get at what was left. I tipped it back, and swallowed the last lump of ice cream.

Keira gave me a sideways look. My wingman, though invisible, was not helping.

"Can you recommend some books about Celtic culture? I really would like to know more about what Rigby and Nessa were into. Maybe it'll help me find out what happened."

"I'd be happy to do that," said Keira.

We finished up and paid. I noticed that I'd shredded my napkin. I held the front door open for Keira.

"Why thank you," she said.

"Think nothing of it. Shall we take a few moments by the water?"

"Certainly."

A few minutes later, Keira and I were sitting on the town pier, dangling our legs over the water. The light wind was calming. A boat-whistle sounded, and a seagull perched nearby flew off.

"Do you mind if I smoke?" asked Keira.

"Only if you give me one."

She retrieved two American Spirits, lit them both and passed me one. For the first time I noticed how nicely the orange flowers set off her black summer dress. If she wore make-up, I couldn't tell. I felt a little lightheaded.

"When you came in the library today, I remembered you from your Da's funeral—I was there with Debbie O'Shea, the singer in your Da's band. They were sweet on each other."

"The singer?"

"Yes."

"I met her at the wake." I wondered if Keira knew about the sloppy kiss. Probably. "I believe there was a boozy kiss between us that night."

"Mmm, she told me."

"Didn't know who she was at the time…"

"No worries—come back to the library with me, I'll give you Keating's history for a start. He's a County Cork man. We can talk about it in a few days."

"I'd love to. Thanks."

Passing the High Tide Gallery, we saw a bright red poster. I looked closer. On the poster was a man's face with a gag over his mouth and three words below, in capital letters: "DON'T TELL ANYONE!"

Keira read from the poster, "Dr. Strange and the Strangelies, Poetry reading and concert. Day after tomorrow."

"I knew those guys growin' up, they toured with Fairport Convention. I was too young to see 'em live back then. I can't believe they're here. Will you come?"

"Wouldn't miss it."

Chapter Thirty

Castletownbere, County Cork, June 4, 2009

Walking toward the harbor, Keira and I heard music coming from an old stone building where fishermen used to offload their catch, but was now the High Tide Gallery—just big enough for twenty-five people to sit for concerts and poetry readings.

A bright green moss grew on the quarried foundation stones, and a delicate ivy with bright purple flowers climbed next to the front door. Keira wore a light green shirt and blue jeans. Her ponytail bounced pleasantly when she turned her head.

It was a half-hour before the concert, and Dr. Strange and the Strangelies were warming up. They played acoustic guitar, piano, flute, violin and drums. Keira and I sat halfway back in the near-empty seats. The lead singer tested his pipes.

I'm bound for Beara the country of my dreams, for the magic land along the Wild Atlantic Way, I've made up my mind, it's where I'm going to stay.

The voice was familiar. Acid-folk. I smiled inside. The other members joined in on the chorus. I leaned close to Keira's ear.

"Back in the late '60s, my Da would have called these guys blow-ins—artists from Cork City or Dublin looking for a life in the country, away from it all. They'd broken up by the time I was five,

173

but man, how cool, they toured Europe with Fairport Convention. I played their albums at college parties. They were like the Irish version of The Incredible String Band."

The group worked on the harmonies of the chorus. *I fell in love at the high tide club, but the tide went out and I was left alone...*

"Let's go outside 'til they're ready," said Keira.

I would have followed her anywhere. I'd spent the night before reading library books. I aimed to impress. We walked toward the pier.

"Keating's story about the other Ark that survived Noah's flood—I didn't realize they landed in Dunmare," I said. "That's only forty miles from here, as the crow flies." We sat at the same spot on the pier as the day before.

"Noah refused the family of Bioth a place on the ark," said Keira, dangling her legs. "So they abandoned the God of Noah, built their own boat, adored their own idol, and survived."

"It's funny how Keating scolded himself for writing down such un-Christian stories." I took the book from my knapsack, and opened to the bookmark. I came prepared. "*It is not to be said that these same people, alive before the flood, would live after it, because the Scripture is against it.*"

"O'Grady did the same thing," said Keira. "He warns his dear readers that Ossianic poetry is the worst in literature, and then relates the dialogue in which Ossian defends the noble ways of the Tuatha Dé Danann with St. Patrick. I'm guessin' Rigby and Nessa were on Ossian's side."

I stood up and offered my hand. She took it, and I helped pull her up. At the gallery, we found two seats near the back. We'd missed one poem. I recognized the Strangelies lead singer Tim Goulding at the microphone, explaining that the next poem came from a woman who preferred not to read in public, dedicated to her mentor, an artist and fisherman who had recently died at sea.

Lately I've been

174

hanging out with the stars
above your house,
looking down on you
everywhere.

Your heart is beating
in the stones,
your words are written
on the waves.

You were made
of here.

I've been listening for you
in the landscape
but when I heard the choughs
kissing the wind
I should have known.

Out of the blue
I see you
courting a cloud.

There was a sheen on Keira's eyes. It reminded me how little
I knew about her. Was she thinking of her father, a sister, a lover?
We weren't young anymore. I got us white wine in see-through
plastic cups.

The room changed when the Strangelies got going—a familiar
mix of traditional wistfulness, and odd-funny late '60s lyrics.
We're oddly strange, but strangely normal. They played *Darksome
Burn*, the traditional *Hames and Thraces* and wrapped up with
Strange World. I tapped my feet.

*People hidin' in the street, throwin' rocks at their brother,
throwin' rocks at you, everybody wants to blame each other...In*

*the time that we live in this world, I really want to know, what
make this strange world go?*

*In the time that I live in this world, there's one thing that I
know. Without love, my heart won't break, my fire won't burn, the
earth won't shake. Without love, what is my destiny? There is no
you and me. Without love, love, love, it's a strange world, a
strange, strange world...*

As the applause died down, Keira tugged at my elbow.

"Are you going to greet them?"

"They don't know me."

"But you're a fan from way back."

"All right then."

"They've gone out the back door. Come on."

Outside, Dr. Strange and the Strangelies posed on the hood of
someone's bright red Mercedes, leaning back against the
windshield and making silly faces. It was either self-effacing
mockery of '60s rock stars, or the next album cover. A pretty
blonde with aviator sunglasses took pictures. Keira shot a few with
her phone just before they got in the Mercedes and drove off,
waving out the windows.

"Looks like we're not invited to the after-party," said Keira.

We went back to the gallery, filled our glasses of wine, and
walked back to what was rapidly becoming our favorite spot on the
pier.

"Why did you leave?"

"Ireland?"

"Yes."

"When I graduated from Cork City, the unemployment rate
was eighteen percent. I was staring down the barrel of inevitable
wretched poverty."

"Is that all?"

"Wretched poverty? No, I always wanted to get out. The
world has its notion of the Irish playin' fiddles, doin' a jig, tellin'
tales of magical faeries and all that shite. To me it felt like a sad

place, like everyone was just waitin' for the next catastrophe to come along."

"Nicely put." We drank and smoked for a few minutes. "In high school, my sister and I made up a board game about relationships. The winner lived happily ever after."

"Like Monopoly, but more meaningful."

"If you landed on "We Have To Talk," you had to pick a card, like Chance in Monopoly. I remember there was "Bad Acne: Miss A Turn," and "Boyfriend Has Body Odor: Pay $5 For Hygiene Products.""

"I always wondered what you gals were up to in your secret meetings."

"Auntie Hannah would play with us—she'd been thrown out of a convent for gettin' knocked up, so she had her bit of wisdom to pass. She was the one told us about Saint Gwen, the three-breasted goddess of nursing mothers."

"Woman of my dreams."

"It frightened me. I imagined three babes goin' at it."

"Didn't think of that."

"Sadly, the abundant Saint Gwen was banished from the church records back in the nineteenth century, though she was still a favorite of Auntie Hannah. It seems her image was not conducive to devotion."

"Depends what kind of devotion."

Keira laughed, which was my goal. Before I could say another funny word, she kissed me on the lips, briefly.

"Good," she said. "That's out of the way."

"I feel much better," I said. "Again?"

The second time, we kissed a little longer, but not so much that arousal was irreversible.

"Now I'm finally comfortable in my skin, it's beginning to wrinkle," Keira said, pinching her arm. "See?"

"You're lovely," I said. "You're beautiful, without a doubt."

"Thank you."

"You're welcome." We got up, and I put my arms around her. We fit just right, her head in the crook of my shoulder. The rigging of ships in the harbor clinked in the damp air.

"Feels nice," she said, into my shoulder.

I tried to kiss her again. She smiled and put a finger on my lips. "Enough for now dearie, I do have rules."

We walked toward the parking lot. It seemed too eager to ask about the rules.

"Do you remember the show, *Wanderly Wagon*?" asked Keira.

"Yeah—the flying wagon—that was a great show, with Judge the dog and Mr. Crow." A couple of gulls squawked over our heads. Waves sloshed between the fishing boats and the pier.

"You remind me of Forty-coats."

"The guy whose coat was made up of forty other coats?"

"Yes."

"Why?"

"Your face is a map of what you're feeling. Guys aren't always like that. It's reassurin'."

"So neither I nor Forty-coats have much of a poker face then."

"No." Keira smiled.

"So you can tell I'd like to see you again, sooner than later."

"I'm sure it can be arranged."

Chapter Thirty-one

Townland of Disert, County Cork, Ireland, September 12, 1916

Rigby stood in the attic of the house where Ness grew up, looking out the little window to the lighthouse. He held the wood cash box that Ness had recovered from the remains of the bookstore.

Inside was a black and white photograph of the young couple and George Russell at Brú na Bóinne, their marriage license, their letters to each other while Rigby was in Egypt and a lock of her rust-orange hair. Rigby closed the box and locked it, placing the key above the little window. He placed the box on the seat of the rocking chair Ness used as a child.

Rigby stood and looked out at the lighthouse. Tears fell down his cheeks. He bowed his head and walked away from the little window.

In the second floor hallway, Rigby picked up the iron post maul he'd left there and swung it like a sledgehammer, shattering the base of the handrail on the pull-down stairs, along with several balusters. He swung again and smashed the first two steps. Another swing, two more steps. He was sweating.

Rigby carefully aimed a fourth swing with the iron post maul, and the rest of the stairs broke loose and crashed to the floor. He set the post maul aside, and stacked the broken pieces of wood. Five-year-old Daniel came up the stairs from the kitchen. Rigby stood up suddenly and dropped a piece of wood to the floor. Daniel turned and ran down the stairs.

Over several trips, Rigby took the remains of the pull-down stairs down to the old stone stable. By sunset, Rigby had used some of the wood to build a sturdy wooden hatch to close off the attic. By sunset, the hatch was installed and screwed shut. From the front porch, Rigby called for his son Daniel twice, then again. Rigby's horse was tied to the oak in the front yard. The house was quiet. Rigby stood in front of the house, and called Daniel's name again.

"Don't be afraid. Seanathair will be home in a few hours. He will take care of you. I know he loves you and you love him. I wish I never left. I see myself signing up for the war…" Rigby's voice resonated in the dampness of the granite hollow. "I missed everything. I was a fool, and because I deserted the Corps, I'm a danger to Gerald and to you. I can't use my own name. Daniel, you can pretend I caught a disease in the war, and wanted to be sure my precious son didn't catch it too."

Rigby saw Daniel looking down from the second floor window. Rigby waved. Daniel waved back. Rigby got on his horse, squeezed its flanks, and was soon at a trot down the two-lane track toward Castletownbere. On the kitchen table, Rigby left the affidavit and a note for Gerald.

Dear Gerald,

I cannot live a life here. We've spoken on the subject enough. I wish of course to bring my son with me and begin again in New York. It has been impossible to face another loss. I look at him and see her eyes, but he is wary of me, even fearful. He associates my arrival back in his short life with his mother's sudden death, and in my agitated state, I've been little help to him.

It's clear enough now. If Daniel and I travel together, and I am arrested, he would have a second parent suddenly taken before his eyes, and he would fall into the hands of the authorities. That cannot happen. I only hope that my absence from his life thus far will make my departure that much easier for him.

In New York City, I believe I can disappear and live without fear. I will contact you by mailing a letter inside a book with the return address of a bookstore in New York. You were a saviour to Nessa and myself, and now for Daniel. I will send money as I can.

R.

Affidavit of Rigby Harold Harrington   April 7, 1917

I, Rigby Harrington, willfully deserted the British Service Corps, No. 7 Labour Company, El Kantara, on July 8, 1915. According to her wishes, I assisted Nessa (O'Dalaigh) Harrington in escaping the Peaumont Sanitorium. She subsequently died of typhoid fever at her birthplace in the Townland of Disert, on July 22, 1915. Nessa was interred in a palace of shimmering crystal amidst the singing of birds, in the cave of the high cliff, so she might come back among us.

*   *   *

In the gathering twilight, Daniel saw the note his father left on the kitchen table. It was addressed to his Seanathair. Daniel knew he wasn't supposed to open envelopes that weren't addressed to him. He stared at it. This envelope was from his father. Daniel snatched it from the table and ran upstairs to his room, where he put it under a floorboard, next to his coins.

Chapter Thirty-two

Dunboy Castle, County Cork, June 7, 2009

"When do I get to hear about the accident?"

"Small town."

"It is."

Keira and I were walking through a pleasant little forest, sloping gently down toward the water, near the harbor mouth. We both had full-on camping backpacks full of food and gear, all carefully planned, mostly by Keira.

"I was driving north on the Wild Atlantic Way, and the sun blinded me. One of those mini-Mack trucks came around a tight corner and I over-steered into a ditch, and flipped into a creek." I told her about T, and bringing him to Ireland, and that he only got a concussion and a torn shoulder, and was now back on Cape Cod, putting up tents.

"They took you to Cork City Hospital?"

182

"By helicopter. I don't remember it. They said I flat-lined for about twenty seconds."

A pair of runners passed us, going down the trail.

"So you had a NDE—my sister had one when we were teenagers; she almost drowned. Afterwards she described seeing her own body from above, and a long tunnel—it's pretty common."

"No lights or tunnels for me." The choppy waters at the harbor mouth came into view as we descended through the trees.

"Do you remember anything?"

"I remember seeing some odd-looking people in the hospital, all dressed in white with white gloves, just standing still and looking at me. I think I knew they weren't real people and they weren't really there. They kept disappearing when I tried to look at their eyes, and then they'd reappear somewhere else. Probably the truckloads of morphine I was on."

The two runners jogged back up the trail and passed us.

"Did you ever see their eyes?"

"Not really, just a little glimpse before they disappeared— they were sort of fishy, like they were wearing goggles."

Keira slipped on wet leaves, and I caught her arm before she fell.

"Thanks." We kept walking. The trail took a right, parallel to the shore. "Was it scary?"

"The ghost-people? Not at first, but when they kept coming back—I don't know, I didn't like them staring at me, I didn't know what they wanted. At some point there was a voice that told me to open my eyes, and breathe, and to eat something and they'd go away, and they did."

"Sounds like what a nurse would say."

"It does."

We stopped to explore an old ruin by the path. It was once a good-sized stone house, but now the walls were two or three feet

high, and they were covered in all sorts of climbing vegetation,
barely recognizable as anything.

A stream running downhill was captured in a stone sluice that
ran through one side of the house and out the other. Water still ran
through it.

"They had running water," I said. "Take the fresh water
coming in for drinking and cooking, and wash up where it runs out
the other side."

"Who needs plumbing when there's a river running through
it," said Keira. We picked our way through the ferns and back to
the trail, which continued meandering along the shoreline. A pair
of black-backed gulls floated overhead, looking for a meal.

"Did you have anxiety?" asked Keira. "Do you mind me
asking all these questions?"

"I don't mind, I kinda like it. I've probably asked several
hundred thousand questions in my job, so it's nice to have it come
back the other way." I sat on the wide trunk of a downed pine, got
out the orange juice, took a swig and offered it to Keira. She drank.
"For a month after the hospital, it felt like something very bad was
about to happen, pretty much every minute, all day. It used to be
that I'd get anxious when there was some reason for it, but this is
different, like a free-floating ball of anxiety that goes where I go."
I took another swig of OJ, screwed the top and put it back in my
knapsack.

"How'r'ya keepin' now?"

We started back on the trail, passing a small field of soft-
yellow buttercups.

"Not so bad as before—it comes and goes now. It's more like
a feelin' of not knowin' what I'm worried about. I no longer expect
a catastrophe at all times."

"Congratulations."

"Thank you."

The path emerged into the stone remains of Dunboy Castle, now just a few walls and a pair of astone archways that appeared ready to crumble.

"This is it," said Keira. "This is where the Siege of Dunboy took place in 1602. The castle was owned by Donal O'Sullivan, chief of Dunboy. It's usually deserted outside of tourist season."

I read a plaque screwed into the ancient stone in 1952, memorializing the 350th anniversary of the Seige. I followed Keira to a flat spot of grass not far from the stone remains.

"They were the last holdouts." said Keira, arranging a red and orange wool blanket on the grass. "They held on for two weeks before the heavy artillery was brought in. Ninety-five people died here and forty-eight more were executed in downtown Castletownbere."

After upacking the plates, utensils, glasses, and napkins, I poured the wine and we tipped our glasses.

"To the last holdouts," said Keira.

"I hope they don't mind us havin' a picnic," I said.

"Well that's more or less what they were fighting for wasn't it?" said Keira, "to have a picnic where you want to and where you want to."

"I suppose so." We were quiet for a moment.

"So what's after journalism?" asked Keira.

"I don't know. I'm at liberty. I'm gonna keep makin' choices I can live with. I was twenty-five years in an office, and now I'm wondering why I kept my nose so damn close to the grindstone."

"You live in Massachusetts."

"I'm not sure where home is. This place is nice. It's where I am."

I got out my mini-boombox and hit play. There was no mistaking the opening of *Tell Me Something Good.* It suddenly felt like the right antidote to the grim history of the place.

"Chaka Khan!" Keira exclaimed, holding out her arms. I took the cue and took her hands. We did our best to slow-dance to the funky beat. *You refuse to put anything before your pride, but what I got will knock your pride aside...*"

Under the influence of Spanish wine, an Irish sunset and Chaka Kahn, we were suddenly both rolling on the wool blanket, kissing and squirming, pushing away clothing like a pair of teenagers.

"Wait, wait." It was Keira's voice. I stopped moving.

"What?"

"No need to rush," she said. "I've found thatg not much good happens when people are all in a rush." Fair enough, I thought.

"Hard not to go for it when the Super Hits of the '70s are playin.'" I said.

Keira smiled and refilled the glasses. I got busy making a small fire in stone-ringed fire pit. When the fire had grown self-sufficient we sat side by side against a mossy boulder and watched the sun join the horizon. The moon was just short of full.

"I miss real fireplaces," said Keira. "Suddenly they're all gone, except for the fake ones you turn on with a switch. I prefer the crackling and popping sounds. You never know when an ember will pop out at you."

The sun dropped below the horizon as one of America's Top '70s Hits came on the boom-box. *Chewin' on a piece of grass, walkin' down the road, tell me how long you gonna stay here, Joe.* A soft rain started to fall. Then the rain started to pick up. We dragged the chairs and the boom box under an enormous tree and huddled together under a blanket.

"Do you mind if I explain something?" asked Keira.

"Go ahead."

"I'm a romantic, which makes me blind."

The rain was softer now, but the wind was picking up. I wasn't sure what to say.

"I've recently discovered I come from a long line of romantics," I said.

186

"I've hoped so badly for a shinin' knight to appear that I can't see who's really standin' there in front of me." The raindrops fell a bit harder.

"And when the mist clears, they're not what you thought," I said. "I've done that sort of thing once or twice. Or more."

"So you see why I put a stop to the dry humpin?" It was getting warm under the wool blanket.

"I do understand, but it doesn't worry me."

"Good. Why?"

"Because I believe it's possible to be a reformed romantic."

"Pray tell?"

"It's when you see people for who they really are, and pretend they're a shining knight."

"A reformed romantic."

"It's the only way."

We kissed, and this time there was no stopping.

Chapter Thirty-three

Townland of Disert, County Cork, Ireland, June 7, 2009

We heard Uncle Fran coming long before we saw him turn the corner into the driveway. He was a confirmed bachelor who loved his old motorbikes, especially the old black and silver Triumph.

"May as well start meetin' the family. Fran's my Da's little brother by eight years."

"I'll make tea."

I met Fran on the porch, and we sat on the wicker chairs. He thanked me for scanning and emailing the old letters.

"When I got 'em, I couldn't stop readin' 'em, and when I was done, I couldn't stop thinkin' about a night with my Da forty years ago, when I was maybe sixteen. Your Da was out of the house then, just got married."

Keira brought out a tray of tea and crackers. After introductions and pleasantries, I brought Keira up to speed, and Fran said what he came to say.

"Da was standin' by that old, half-rusted oil barrel at the bottom of the field, burnin' garbage, an' I could see he wasn't standin' straight so much as managin' to stay upright. Mum was havin' no part of 'im in those days, but I was worried about 'im. He wasn't a mean drunk so much as a solitary one.

"So I went down the field, and saw he had some papers in his hand, starin' at the fire. He always looked ten years older than 'e was, and 'is teeth were yellowin' from tobacco. He always had the pipe in 'is breast pocket, stickin' up out of it.

"I asked if he's gonna burn the papers in his hand, and he says no, he likes to read by the fire. I stood with 'im for a while, starin' at the fire and wishin' I hadn't come down the field. I was about to leave, and asked if there was somethin' I could do for 'im, could I 'elp 'im. He smiled at me, which 'e never did, and gave me the crumpled papers in 'is hand. 'Maybe you can,' he says to me, and looks back at the fire."

Fran took a piece of folded paper from his pocket and handed it to me. The paper had been folded, crumpled and stained, but the ink was clear enough. There was one short paragraph. I read it out loud.

"Affidavit of Rigby Harold Harrington. I, Rigby Harrington, willfully deserted the British Service Corps, No. 7 Labour Company, El Kantara, on July 8, 1915. According to her wishes, I assisted my wife, Nessa Harrington in escaping the Peamount Sanitarium, and transported her to the Townland of Disert, her birthplace. She subsequently died on July 22, 1915. Nessa was interred in a palace of shimmering crystal amidst the singing of birds, in the cave of the high cliff, so she might come back among us. Rigby Harold Harrington, April 7, 1917."

I folded the letter and handed it back to Fran.

"Did you tell Da about it?"

"Nah."

"Why not?"

"It was so long ago I don't really remember, maybe there was somethin' I liked 'bout knowin' things my brother didn't."

"Excuse me," said Keira. We both turned to look at her. "Interred in a palace of shimmering crystal?" she said. "In a cave of the high cliff?"

"Do you think Nessa's really buried in a cave?" I asked.

"Rigby seems like a pretty serious fellow," said Kiera.

"There's a lot of high cliffs around," said Fran, handing me another folded piece of paper. "Here's somethin' else." It was Rigby's handwriting, a short letter addressed to Nessa's father, dated September 15, 1916. I read it out loud.

"Dear Gerald. As you know, I cannot live a life here. We've spoken on the subject many times. I wish of course to bring my son with me and begin again in New York. It has been impossible for me to face another loss. I look at him and see Nessa. But Daniel is wary of me, even fearful. He connects my arrival with his mother's sudden death, and in my agitated state, I've been little help.

"It's clear enough now. If Daniel and I travel together, and I am arrested, he would have a second parent suddenly taken before his eyes, and he would fall into the hands of the authorities. That cannot happen. I only hope that my absence from his life thus far will make my departure that much easier for him. In New York City I can disappear, and live without fear. I will contact you by mailing a letter inside a book with the return address of a bookstore in New York. You were a saviour to Nessa and myself, and now for Daniel. I will send money as I can. Signed, R."

The room was quiet.

"So Rigby went to New York," I said.

"After burying Nessa in a cave," said Keira, walking over to the bookcase.

"Right," I said.

"Anyone thinkin' what I'm thinkin'?" she asked, pulling an old book from the top shelf.

"There might still be a letter inside a book?" said Fran. "Don't bother yourself, I've looked through 'em all."

"What about *Cormac's Glossary,* the copy Rigby left in the attic?"

"I checked it – no old letters or money inside." Fran handed Keira the old book. "It's Nessa's copy – she signed her name before the title page."

"I read through it after getting back from the hospital," I said.

"It's a glossary," said Keira flipping through the book. "Did ya like it?"

"Sure. I didn't know any of the words."

Keira stopped flipping.

"There's notes in the margins here and there," said Keira. "There's a star drawn in pencil next to the entry about Disert." She peered closely at the mark in the book. "Looks old."

"Wasn't me," I said. "I wouldn't write in an old book."

Keira read the entry next to the star.

"'Disert: Though barren now, a great house was there before.' The note below says the word 'stripped' is an alternate meaning for 'barren.'"

"Didn't they strip turf to build mounds?" I asked.

Keira nodded.

"So where you find stripped turf, you find mounds," I said.

"Let's assume Nessa put the star in the glossary," said Keira. "Maybe she went lookin' for the great house that was there before. If we're thinkin' Rigby left the box and *Cormac's Glossary* in the attic, he must have had a reason for it."

"Maybe Nessa found something," I said.

"Maybe she did," said Fran.

"Like a cave in a high cliff," said Keira. "Caves were considered entrances to Tír na nÓg."

"There's caves in the cliffs all along the coast," said Fran. "The tallest cliffs in Disert are out past Paddy's pastures, by Murtogh's Cove."

191

"What say we get up there tomorrow," I said. "Poke around a bit. Bring some lunch."

"I'll call Paddy and let him know we're comin' through," said Fran. "How are you two with dirt bikes?"

"I'm healed up enough," I said. "Ready to break somethin' else."

Chapter Thirty-four

Townland of Disert, County Cork, June 15, 2009

The next morning, equipped with food and beverages, a camp shovel and Fran's metal detector, we walked single-file up an old switch-backing path with Fergus and Paddy leading the way.

Paddy hadn't thought much of dirt bikes disturbin' his sheep, but he was game to come along for the walk. He said the highest cliff was out past the three standing stones beyond the north edge of his property. We met on the promontory where the Atlantic was spread out below. I'd taken the last of the Dilaudid before we left, and chose a sturdy walking stick. After sayin' our hellos, we got walking up a single-track to the north, through endless rose hip bushes, showing their first flowers. The path switch-backed up a steady grade for ten minutes. We emerged into a grassy area within sight of the Atlantic, and a set of limestone cliffs to the north.

"Trail's end," said Paddy. "The high cliffs are there."
Between us and the high ridges was a sea of rose hip, gorse and
short, knotty scrub oak.

"So that's why you told us to wear wool," I said.

"I've not bothered goin' that way," said Paddy. "I'm not
much for wadin' through gorse. You'll want to find a game trail if
ya can."

"We should've brought a machete," said Keira.

It was Fergus who found the way—a game trail just wide
enough to shuffle through, twisting and ducking with every step. I
put the walking stick to good use, doing all I could to clear the way
for Keira. The occasional rabbit flushed from the underbrush, and
calling birds fled the bushes.

Behind Keira was Fran, and Paddy at the rear somewhere, at
his own pace. The panting Fergus ran a constant loop, exploring up
ahead and then returning, running past everyone to check on
Paddy. Then it was up ahead again. I stubbed my toe on something
hard. It was a smooth stone of white quartz. I showed it to Keira.

"That's a water-rolled stone."

Fran looked it over. "Doesn't belong up here," he said. He
looked around. "There's another."

We followed the game trail, finding two more smooth white
stones underfoot, each about the size of a large fist. After a few
minutes, the bushes thinned out. The ground was sandier, with
clumps of grass here and there. We picked our way through a
jumble of rocks to the highest point on the ridge, behind the high
cliff. The wind from the ocean was damp and salty. The sea
sparkled.

"Look!" Keira pointed. There was an opening in the brush we
hadn't seen from below. It was sandy and roughly circular, about
twenty feet across. I could see white stones in the sand.

"This whole area could have been stripped," said Keira, as we
made our way to the opening. "The bushes thin out, and now

there's a bare spot. If you were going to build a great house, you'd build it up here."

"The monks sure loved the coast," said Fran. "I was always told they tended fires and rang bells to warn sailors in the fog."

There was no hint of a structure, no foundation stones or old walls. The cool wind dried the sweat on my face and neck.

"Is that a sinkhole?" said Fran. At the edge of the clearing was a hole in the sandy soil, roughly oval, about six inches deep, just enough to notice. I poked in the hole and hit something hard. I poked again, a few inches away. It felt like a rock. Another poke. *Click.*

Fran got out the camp shovel and cleared away the sandy soil, exposing a flat slab of gray granite. "That's quarried," said Fran. He slid the shovel under the thin slab, and leveraged it upwards a few inches. I grabbed an edge and together we slowly flipped it aside.

Keira dropped a stone into the opening. It quickly clattered on the bottom. "Couldn't be more than ten feet," she said.

Fran tied off a rope on the nearest outcrop of rock, and tossed it into the hole.

"Paddy?" he offered.

"I believe I'll stand by. Might offer words of wisdom, as needed."

Fran took the rope, and carefully rappelled down the hole. "The sides are cut stone," he said. "Oh. I'm on the bottom. It's not deep."

"Waddya see?" I asked.

"There's a passage," Fran said, clearing stones and dirt. "I'm not fittin' through." Fran pulled himself up on the rope, and I gave him a last boost out of the hole. He put his hands on my shoulders. "You might fit."

I took hold of the rope and sort-of slid down the side of the hole. The walls were quarried stone stacked on top of each other. The passage was carved out of white limestone, almost two feet in diameter. I felt around for a crevice, pulled myself in and twisted myself forward. A sharp edge cut into my ribs, and I squirmed away from it. I stopped moving and took as full a breath as I could, let it all out and pushed forward. It was inch by inch. Let out the breath; squirm forward. Finally, the passage grew wider. I could see sunlight.

I crawled out of the passage into a cave. About thirty feet in front of me was an opening in the cliff-side, letting sunlight in at a slant, sparkling on the white quartz that littered the floor. I stood up as Keira emerged from the passage. We were quiet. Outside of the angled shafts of sunlight, the cave darkened.

We walked to the opening and looked out over the dark-blue ocean. Seagulls circled and called. The cliff dropped almost straight down, about three hundred feet to the rocky beach.

Keira flicked on her boxy flashlight, and we turned toward the cave. Smooth, water-rolled quartz stones covered the floor, catching the light. We walked toward the back of the cave, which opened up to the left. The flashlight showed a pile of stacked granite slabs, about four feet high. Lying on top were the bones of a small child, partly covered by something old and tattered.

"It's a wing," whispered Keira. "A big one." The remains of white feathers lay on the child's skeleton.

"A swan's wing," I said. "Takin' the child to Tír na nÓg."

We stood quietly. After a minute, Keira moved the flashlight away. There was
still the other side of the dark cave to see.

"You take it," she said, handing me the flashlight. We picked our way between the round white stones on the floor, and the flashlight lit up the far wall. There were three spirals, each one above the other. Shining the flashlight down, the beam fell on a skeleton in the remnants of a white dress. Keira and I stopped still.

She lay on a bed of smooth white stone, propped up against the cave wall, reclining. Her bright orange hair lay over her shoulders and down to her waist.

"It's Nessa," whispered Keira.

The room brightened as the angling sunlight moved toward the back of the cave. A small bird flew in, preened itself for a moment, and flew out. The sunbeams reached the top of the far wall, above Nessa. The light gently descended, lighting up the highest spiral etched in the cave wall, then the spiral below it, and finally the third.

"Like it's telling a story," whispered Keira.

When the sun fell on Nessa, her hair brightened, and her bed of quartz glowed softly. By her side, half hidden under dirt and sand, I saw a leather journal, wrapped tightly in twine. Two bony fingers lay over one corner.

I made my way around the body for a closer look. I kneeled down by Nessa's side. *Take it.* I blew sand off the cover of the journal. All I could make out was "A Pri...he...tur...ons."

I took hold of the journal and slowly slid it away from the fingers, which clicked on the stone below.

"Thanks, Nessa," I whispered.

The sun steadily retreated from the bones of my great-grandmother, moving slowly across the floor. When the sunlight hit the clear crystal inset into the floor, beams of color flew around the cave.

Keira squeezed my hand. I put my arm around her shoulder. It was like fireworks close-up. Then it was over. The sunbeams crawled backward and out of the cave. We stood still, staring out the opening.

"That's happened every sunny day for a hundred years," I said.

"If all went right, she rode those sunbeams out of here long ago," said Keira.

"Wha'd ya find in there!" It was Paddy's voice, coming through the passage.

Keira and I looked at each other.

"What're we s'posed to tell 'im?" I asked.

People of the Flow

"That we found a way to Tír na nÓg."

Chapter Thirty-five

New York City Public Library, 5ᵗʰ Avenue, July 1, 2009

Entering the Rose Main Reading room is like entering a church. It's three feet short of a football field in length, seventy-eight feet wide and the gilded ceiling is fifty-two feet above the floor. Sun streamed through the massive, arch-shaped windows that paraded along both walls. Beats the hell out of Google.

There were a half-a-dozen Harold Harringtons in the 1920 Census for New York City: three in the Bronx, two in Queens and one in Manhattan. The one in Manhattan was the right age; thirty-four. My pulse picked up. Was it him? He lived at 16 Van Nest Place, #2. I got out a street map but couldn't find Van Nest Place.

Having somehow equated librarians with nuns at a young age, I had to fight against the involuntary impulse to look at my shoes as I approached.

"I can't seem to find a Van Nest Place in Manhattan, and I suspect it doesn't exist anymore. I'm not sure how to go about finding the new name, and where it is."

"Street necrology," said the elderly woman with short brown hair. "One moment." Her nametag said Margaret. After a minute of tapping, she looked up.

"They changed the name of the street in 1936—it's Charles Street now, between Bleeker and West Fourth." I looked blank. "In the Village."

"Thanks." My deductive reasoning centers were still a work in progress, and my ability to hold more than one thing in my head at once was still temporarily off-line. I needed help.

"Do you have a minute?"

"Certainly."

I told Margaret my story, and what I knew about Harold Harrington. Like any good librarian, she joined the chase. Efficiently.

"Bookstore owner in Dublin, arrives after 1915, living near the village in 1920…That's when Bookseller's Row was just starting up on Fourth Avenue, south of Union Square. If he was in the book business, he might have gotten work in one of those early stores."

"Are they still there?"

Margaret frowned. "Sadly no. Just The Strand."

"When did they open?" Tap, tap. "1927." Tap, tap, tap. "Schulte's Bookstore was the first—they opened up in 1919, at Fourth and Tenth." Tap, tap, tap. "They specialized in theological books from around the world, many of them quite old. They bought entire collections."

"Aha!" There was a faint hint of a smile on Margaret's face.

"Are we having a moment?"

"Sounds like a place where Harold would work. I've tried to search online for marriage licenses, birth and deaths, but I'm a bit of a dinosaur in that regard."

Margaret was already typing. Sweat beaded on my forehead. Tap, tap, tap. She picked up the phone and talked to someone very quietly. Only librarians can whisper that way. Finally she stood up.

"Follow me, please."

We walked down a set of marble stairs, through a modern set of double doors, down a long hallway and into a large room full of standing bookshelves. Margaret retrieved a heavy, old municipal book, placed it on a conference table, opened it about halfway, and flipped through several pages. I got out my notebook and sat down.

"Birth record for Gerald Harrington. 1923. Father Harold Harrington, mother Johanna (Sullivan) Harrington, 16 Van Nest Place."

"So he married again. Any other children?"

"No."

"Did Gerald marry?"

"The records after 1930 are on computer," she said, sitting down at an old PC, which hummed when she turned it on. Tap, tap, tap. "Gerald married Anna Ludwig on March 12, 1940. One child, Molly Harrington, born January 6, 1940."

"That adds up nicely. What happened to Gerald?" Tap, tap, tap. "Missing in action over Germany, 1943." Tap, tap, tap. "Anna died in 2005."

"And Molly?"

"She never married. The last census has her at 1143 Houston Street, Apt. 401."

I looked up. "Really?"

Margaret smiled.

"Really."

*　　　　　*　　　　　*

1143 Houston Street was a classic old five-story brick apartment building with rounded gables, a small patch of front yard and an iron fence running the length of the block.

Should I really just show up, or would an email be better to start out? A phone call? Who shows up on the doorstep anymore? The answer came back. Family.

The iron gate was open. The fourth name on the outside buzzer was Molly Harrington. The wind was brisk.

Bzzzzzzz. I stood back. The intercom crackled.

"Hello?" It was a female voice.

"Molly Harrington?"

"Is it a package?" The voice sounded young.

"No. I'm here to…I think I'm a relative."

There was a pause. The intercom crackled.

"Come on up."

Bzzzzzzz.

I opened the door and rode an old, sliding-door elevator to the fourth floor. Down the hall, I knocked on 401. The door opened on a chain. I saw part of a woman in a t-shirt, shorts and sneakers.

"May I have your name?" She had long brown hair and brown eyes, maybe in her late twenties.

"John Harrington." I gave her my Massachusetts driver's license through the small opening in the door. "I think Molly's grandfather was my great-grandfather." I heard a deep sigh on the other side of the door. The lock slid off and the door opened.

"I'm Ensig." We shook hands and she ushered me into the kitchen. She was tall. "Please. Sit." I sat.

"Can I get you something? Tea?" She had some kind of Scandinavian accent.

"Sure, thank you." She turned on the burner under a teapot.

"Why do you come here?" As I told her the story, Ensig assembled a plate of sugar cookies and poured the tea, interrupting only to determine my preferences. Milk and sugar.

I started with finding the letters, proceeded through the bombing of Rigby's shop, his desertion on learning of Nessa's illness, breaking her out of the sanitarium with George Russell, taking her back to the Beara for a pagan burial that was very much off the Parish books, and finally Uncle Fran's long-held story of Rigby leaving his son behind and fleeing to New York City. I ended with Margaret, the reference librarian.

"Wow."

"Yes."

"I'm sorry to tell you that Molly died three weeks ago, from cancer."

I shook my head. "Three weeks?"

"Yes—the condo people want her stuff out. I live upstairs. She has no one. So I pack her things. Not much to anyone, her sketches, the journals where she was published. She was a biologist." She took a cigarette from a packet on the table. "Do you mind?"

"No." She lit the cigarette.

"Did Molly mention a grandfather?"

"Yes, there's a picture." Ensig left the room for a moment, her feet making no sound, and returned with a black and white photo in a frame. It was Rigby. Much older than the photo at Brú na Bóinne.

Ensig looked at the picture, and at me.

"You look something like him. The eyes."

"So I've been told." Ensig took a drag with one hand and dipped a sugar cookie in her tea with the other. I wasn't sure I could do that.

"Her father died when she was little, so he was her favorite grandpa, you know."

I dunked a sugar cookie in my tea.

"Ah!" Ensig snapped her fingers above her head. "There is movie!" I looked up from the sugar cookie. "Sixteen millimeter. Come." I followed Ensig to the living room. She took a reel from a bookshelf and handed it to me.

"This. Last New Year's Eve. She was sick by then. I had dumped my boyfriend. I brought wine to her door. There is a projector, yes." An old sixteen mm projector was under a table

203

behind the couch. On a piece of masking tape half peeled from the reel, it said, "Iceland w/Grandpa, 10/30/61"

"Would you like to see?"

"Yes, please, if you don't mind."

"OK." Ensig put on the reel while I hung a sheet from a bookcase. "Ready." I turned off the lamp.

Molly and Rigby were standing on a rocky beach, well bundled up. Molly had a long brown ponytail. Rigby wore a long pea coat. He had a full white beard and wore a New York Giants baseball cap. 1961. He must have been about seventy-five.

The camera moved down the beach and refocused in the distance, showing dozens of swans bugling and honking. After going white for a few seconds, the same view came on screen, but there were more swans, more than fifty, and the sound track was louder. The camera swung back to show Molly and Rigby on the shoreline. Molly was taking notes. After going white briefly, the screen showed the swans again, but this time they were flapping their wings, jumping, bugling and…dancing. Or, something like dancing.

Over a few minutes they increased the pace of their movements, faster and faster in a frenzy of pumping necks and flapping wings. A dozen swans lifted out of the water and seemed to run over the water, finally lifting off to the southeast, where the camera followed their flight until they were out of sight. The camera moved back to show another wedge of swans taking off in the same direction. The camera swung back to Molly and Rigby on the beach. Molly was jumping up and down, with her fists in the air. Rigby was smiling. The movie clicked off. I stared at the screen.

"Would you like the movie?"

"Yes." I stood up. "Thank you."

"And sketches and journals?"

"Yes, that'd be brilliant, thank you." We shook hands.

"I'm happy. They go where they should go. Oh, wait!"

Ensig rushed out of the room and returned with what looked like a white gift box, not quite tall enough for a bottle of wine. "She always had this in the living room. She said it used to have her Grandpa's ashes."

"Used to?"

"Not anymore. Molly said she spread them somewhere, but it should go with her other things."

Ensig kissed me goodbye on both cheeks, I walked down to the street and hailed a taxi. I don't remember anything about the cab ride, only that it got me to the motel.

*   *   *

I love the anonymity of cheesy motels. The puce green hallways, the faint odor you can't quite place, the glum midnight manager and the rattling air conditioner, preferably augmented by a close-up view of a highway off-ramp, complete with squealing jake brakes.

There was no room service at the Super Duper Eight, so I made do with a chocolate bar, peanuts and an orange Fanta. I picked up Molly's white box and removed the top. Bits of ash were stuck to the sides and the bottom. Inside were two pieces of paper, folded like a letter. I opened it and blew away the bits of ash caught in the creases, and sat down in a comfy chair under a light. The letter was typed.

June 5, 1963

Grandpa's ashes were in the white box in my backpack, and we headed out on a bright Saturday morning to Lake Ridge Lakes, about fifteen miles east of Pockinaw, the last three on a dirt road along the Thompson River drainage.

205

It had been almost two weeks since Grandpa died. I didn't know quite what to think about his ashes. I knew I wanted to bring them to Lake Ridge Lakes because we had picnicked there every year. The path zig-zagged up a steady grade, through a mature beech forest to a series of three little ponds.

As I hiked up the trail, images of Grandpa came to mind—he was walking up ahead, disappearing around a corner for a few minutes, then appearing again, looking back to see where I was. This time, as I turned the corner and came over the rise, there was no sweet old man standing on the shore, feeding the ducks.

New images came.

Grandpa had passed on to the Other World, and he was among the people he'd loved in his life. He was talking with them. I couldn't hear what they were saying, but somehow I knew.

Grandpa was telling his friends about me, saying I had been through a lot of pain, that I was a good woman, and kind. He was telling them to look out for me, and they were nodding their heads and smiling: "*We will.*"

I started to cry. I thought I was there to wish Grandpa a safe journey and a blissful rest. It never occurred to me that he would be looking out for me instead.

I sat on a smooth, rounded rock at the edge of the lake and wiped the tears away.

I took the plastic bag out of the little white box, and poured his ashes back into the box. I thought I should just throw them out all at once into the pond, but I just sat for a while. By that time, I was talking to Grandpa like I used to, and I suggested we take one last walk around the ponds, so I put the little white box in my backpack.

The summer before was a bad drought year, and the ponds had shrunk to about half their normal size. But it had been a good winter for snow, and there was plenty of rain during the spring. The marshes around the edges of the ponds were bright green again.

I stood on the shore behind the last pond of the three ponds, and looked back. There was a cloud in the sky with two bright spots for eyes, a puffy, white nose and a funny, long chin. Maybe Grandpa was up there, maybe he wasn't, but it really didn't matter: I heard a little voice that said, "Look! There are so many beautiful things in this world to play with!"

The little bright spots disappeared and the cloud slowly changed shape. I thought again of Grandpa telling all his friends in the Other World about me, and to look out for me, and that it was even safer now to *just go out and play*.

I walked around the other side of the three ponds, finally approaching the beginning again. Little raindrops started falling, sending ripples over the pond. I stood on an old log at the shoreline and threw his ashes out of the little, white box in one quick motion.

They made a long straight trail of white in the water, bright against the green, underwater plants. As the cloudy ashes dissolved, they spread out with the slow current. Grandpa loved to swim, his long arms neatly cutting the water. As I watched, the ashes spread, I thought, *just keep going*.

After standing on that log, crying and watching Grandpa's ashes settle into the pond, I told all the little plants and flies and the little brown ducks to care for him, and that he would take care of them too, and that I would be back to visit.

Finally I stepped off the log, put the little empty white box in my backpack, and headed back down the trail.

Molly Harrington

Chapter Thirty-six

Cork City College Arts Center, County Cork, December 17, 2009

It had been almost six months, but the deal was almost done. As part of the hundredth anniversary of the Celtic Revival, Cork City College was producing a new, permanent exhibit. Keira and I approached the curator, Sally Flannery, with the seven old letters, including Nessa's mythic prequel to the Tuatha Dé Danann's arrival in Ireland, the photograph of Rigby, Nessa and George Russell at Brú na Bóinne, discrete photos of the rainbow effect in the cave of the high cliff, the sixteen mm film taken in Iceland, Molly's writings on the whooper, Nessa's lock of hair, the journal found in the cave of the high cliff, and three fragments from an ancient manuscript found in its pages. Although the pieces of vellum were charred, making it difficult to establish a date of origin, Flannery was sold.

"Brilliant," she had said, pushing away from her desk. "These artifacts capture the sentiment of the Celtic Revival period quite beautifully—a full expression of the emotional content inherent in the re-emergence of the Gaelic language, and the embracing of Celtic legend and culture."

The details of turning everything over to the college had proved somewhat elusive. The board of trustees didn't share my enthusiasm quite enough to pay a price equal to building a new house on the family property. It was a Friday afternoon, and I was back in Flannery's office for a third meeting. This time, Keira was back at the library in Castletownbere. Flannery's desktop was neatly arranged. She tapped her pen on the table-top.

"The college plans to package the letters and the single photograph with historically contextual materials, providing a personal story against the background of the times," said Flannery, now clicking her pen on and off. "The college also wishes to incorporate Nessa's journal into a new text on pre-Christian religious beliefs. As agreed, you are entitled to half the net revenue from such publications, including digital media, but we are prepared, and would prefer, to purchase your interest in that revenue stream up-front." She slid a piece of paper across the desk.

"A new text on pre-Christian religions," I said. "Nessa would like that."

I turned over the piece of paper. With the sale of Da's shop and apartments, the figure was enough to rebuild on the family property. I had picked out a small plateau just below the ridgeline for a building site, where we'd be able to see the ocean from the second floor. As for the old place, Fran was lobbying the fire department to use it for a practice burn.

I added up the figures in my head again, for the hundredth time. This time, there was enough left over for a trip to New York, and a vacation somewhere beautiful with Keira.

"It's all yours," I said, standing up. Flannery smiled and we shook hands.

Chapter Thirty-seven

Townland of Disert, County Cork, June 11, 2010

Keira and I sat on the slightly tilted front porch in Disert, going through Molly's papers. A squall had just poured rain for a few minutes before moving on. The greens were greener. The air was fresh. The tea was hot.

"So, Rigby, using the name Harold Harrington, married Ellen Hartnett in New York City, in 1920," said Keira, taking notes. "They had a son Geoffrey in 1922, who married Catherine Sullivan in 1940—they have a daughter, Molly, in 1941, and in 1944, Geoffrey is killed flying bombing raids over Germany."

"Right," I said, blowing on the tea.

"And the census records show Catherine and Molly moved in with Rigby and Ellen near Greenwich Village after the war." She made another note. I sipped the tea.

"Rigby must have told Nessa's story to Molly, about the whooper swans and the Tuatha Dé Danann," I said. "Maybe a bedtime story."

"Molly goes to Columbia University and gets a bachelor's in biology, and her graduate degree in field studies of the whooper swan in Iceland," said Keira.

"Which hadn't been studied up to that point," I added.

Keira flipped through one of the *Animal Behavior* journals where Molly's work was published and started reading one of her articles.

"The whooper's nest is nine feet across and three feet high. They use the same nest year after year, unless they're swept away by a flood, which happens occasionally, given their fondness for estuaries."

"A summer home and a winter home."

"Returning to Iceland in early spring, with snow still on the ground," Keira continued. "The mass of organic material making up the nest steams from internally generated heat, often causing the whooper nests to emerge first from the snow cover." She showed me a black and white photo in the journal, showing a swan tending its nest, which steamed in the cold air.

I picked up another edition of *Animal Behavior*, finding another article.

"The greeting ceremony is elaborate and lengthy," I read. "It includes perfect antiphonal calling, when a swan matches the changing duration and tone of the notes, singing them back exactly. After the duet is complete, they flap their wings and rush together." I showed her a picture of two swans standing opposite each other, calling.

"We should have a greeting," I said.

"Are you going to sing every time we meet?"

"I feel like singing every time we meet."

She kissed me.

"Sweet," I said. "More tea?"

"Yes, please."

Keira followed me into the kitchen and continued reading.

"There's a list of different vocalizations. The whooper sings a double note that accompanies its wing-beats. During the day, the flock converses in short, high-pitched tones, and at night they twitter and trill in softer tones. The alarm sound is *Kloo! Kloo!*

And finally, my new favorite—harmonious monosyllabic calls while swimming."

"I can see that being fun," I said.

Keira looked ahead in the article, muttering to herself as her finger slid down the columns of words: "Females mature faster, no surprise, extensive courtship displays in the spring, pairs last up to fourteen years…" Her finger slid down near the end of the page and stopped. The kettle was working up to a whistle. I poured the water, and we headed back out to the front porch. Keira kept reading.

"Before the whoopers take off for the fall migration from Iceland to Ireland, they perform a dance and call, which steadily accelerates in pace until reachin' a frenzied cacophony, during which migration begins, and the birds take off in wedges." We sat down.

"That sounds like Nessa's Song of Flying, before the migration," I said. "She wrote in one of the letters that the early Icelanders thought the swans were super-natural—that they flew to Valhalla for the winter."

"How'd Nessa know about the dancin' I wonder," said Keira, dipping her teabag in and out of the steaming tea.

"Maybe from Brú na Bóinne—the whoopers still winter there now. Maybe they do the same dance when they migrate north in the spring. Nessa and Rigby and George were up there often enough." I lit a cigarette, which goes perfectly with spicy chai. I was way down from the pack-a-day I went through weaning off morphine, but I wasn't quits yet.

Keira read from one of the journals. "Outside their normal winter range, the whooper swan has been spotted around the Mediterranean, and in especially severe winters, in Egypt and North Africa-- "

"Hold on, that reminds me—I got an email this morning from the geneticist from Trinity I met on the plane—I sent her scans of the letters." I put the cigarette in the ashtray, got out my laptop and opened the email.

"Here, she says: 'On one point, I must tell you that Nessa's reading of the legends may have been partially correct. We recently sequenced the genome of DNA taken from the bones of a farmer excavated near Belfast in 1855, and three others buried on Rathlin Island in County Antrim, and determined that a population from the Middle East came to Ireland as farmers around 3,750 B.C., and later interbred with a fair-skinned and blue-eyed population coming from the Pontic steppe of southern Russia, circa 2,300 B.C.E.'"

I retrieved the cigarette. "So, the old legends were right about Brú na Bóinne being built by people with a dark, or brown complexion. It was built about 500 years after the Middle Eastern farmers arrived."

Keira stood up, and started walking slowly back and forth on the porch. I had come to know it as her thinking mode.

"And the Tuatha Dé Danann," she said, turning around at the far end of the porch.

"Excuse me, the People of the Flow, whether they came from Iceland or the Pontic Steppes, they came across the mound at Brú na Bóinne one way or the other, and sort of adopted it. It became the setting for their most important stories."

"In Nessa's story, the Danann's knew it was a winter solstice temple when they first found it," I said, stubbing out the butt. "You said the whoopers got as far as Egypt and North Africa—wasn't there a bird migration map in one of these?"

We both picked up a journal and flipped through the pages. I was on my fourth journal when I found the map.

"Look," I said, showing it to Keira. "A nice, big arrow starting in Central Europe and going south, right down the Nile and the Temple at Karnak. It's called the Adriatic Flyway, from Central Europe to the Sudan."

213

"Gotcha," said Keira, who resumed her slow pacing. A series of taps and finger swooshes later, she showed me a layout of the Temple of Mut, next to the Temple of Karnak.

"See the shallow pool? They could have heated that pool to make steam, and attracted the whoopers—it's documented that swans were domesticated in ancient Egypt."

I'd been wondering how to bring up the idea of taking a vacation together.

"What do you say to spending a week in Egypt?" Keira didn't miss a beat.

"There's precautions on travel there because of the H1N1 flu. People have died."

"How about India? Rigby's homeland. Check out winter grounds for migratory birds."

Keira sat down, tapped on her phone, squinted, and tapped some more.

"I think I got something." Tap, tap, swoosh, tap, tap. "Orissa. The Bay of Bengal." Tap, tap, finger-swoosh. "Biggest winter ground for migratory birds in India. Off the tourist-track, laid-back culture." Tap, tap, tap, swoosh. "There's a lovely little eco-resort on a very wide and sandy beach." More tapping and swooshing.

"Oh!" Keira smiled and started squirming.

"What?"

"There's a sun temple dedicated to the winter solstice."

"You're kidding?"

"Nope. Wanna know what it's called?"

"Yes."

"Konark."

I stared at her. She stared at me.

"That makes three," I said. "Carnac in Brittany, Karnak in Egypt, and now Konark in India. What does it mean—the word Konark?"

Keira tapped rapidly. I could barely see her fingers moving.

"Sun in the southeast corner. The winter solstice."

"And there's a winter ground for migratory birds there?"

"The biggest in India."

Chapter Thirty-eight

Bhubaneswar, India, January 11, 2010

My face was glued to the window for most of the flight
from Delhi to Bhubaneswar, on the northeast coast of India. I
watched the Ganges winding through the green countryside, and
the dome-like rising hills of the Chota Nagpur Plateau. Until that
day, my airplane experience was mostly flying over the Atlantic at
night.

With a few emails and phone calls, Keira had found a fellow
librarian in Odissa who was more than happy to meet us at the
Konark Sun Temple for a guided tour the next day.

All we had was our carry-on, making for a quick trip through
the small airport to a line of taxis, in various states of dilapidation.
No one was sweating the dents around here. The travel books
described a friendly, "laid-back" culture.

Passing several bicycle rickshaws, our taxi headed out of
Bhubaneswar for the sixty-four kilometer drive to the tiny village
of Konark. I had happily consented to staying at the only eco-
resort in the area, right on the beach, but remained uncertain as to
the creature comforts.

"You do realize there's a hotel by the railway station back in town with a private balcony, flat screen TV, free wifi, and free mini-bar items," I said. "I admit the items are not specified, but there's air conditioning, a free newspaper and free parking." Keira politely ignored me, which was ok. At least I got to say my piece. She read from her tablet.

"Located on the northeast coast of India, the Bay of Bengal is fed by the melt waters of the Himalayas. Once located on the coast, the Konark Sun Temple now stands half a mile inland. It was built in the thirteenth century, and declared a World Heritage Site by UNESCO in 1984. World traveler and broadcaster Lowell Thomas said Konark was, quote, 'the most beautiful and the most obscene building in the world.'"

We passed a group of women walking in colorful attire.

"Before we leave, I'm buying you some of those clothes," I said.

"I'd like that." We passed a sign reading, *Chandaka Forest and Elephant Sanctuary,* and turned to each other.

"On the way back," I said.

"Brilliant," she said.

After forty minutes on the road, Keira's need for intermittent food guided us to a stop at the only dhaba in the tiny village of Pipli. We sat outside under a makeshift orange tent, and watched a pair of cows amble across the square. The food, mostly vegetarian, was deliciously spicy.

"Do you remember the first meal we had at the butcher shop?" asked Keira.

"I do."

"Your table habits were closer to a famished medieval knight than a modern man. It made me wonder."

"Really? Am I doing it now?"

"Not so much." The smiling waiter came by and refilled our ice water. "Not like that first time."

I hadn't told her about the big Viking yet.

"It's kinda hard to explain."

"So there's something to it."

"After the ghost-people went away in the ICU, and I started eating, and I must have had one of those dreams that didn't seem like a dream. There was sort of a person, a very big man with leather clothes, and I thought it was me, but it wasn't. It was like I was watching him." I told her about the boat, the priestess, baiting the priest in the tower until he came out and then killing him.

"How did the big Viking kill the priest?"

"With a broadsword to the top of his head. Why?"

"You didn't really kill anyone."

"No."

"So it's OK."

Keira oohed and aahed over the vegetarian khumi, and took a drink of water.

"There've examined the bones of the priests the Vikings killed," said Keira. "They died by a sword to the top of the head."

"No."

"Yes. What happened after you killed him?" I took a drink of cool water.

"I wasn't sure if the woman with me was my queen so much as we were equals. Afterwards, she asked whether I wanted to be different than my brothers, my father and the rest of my family, and I said yes. She said I should bend the river of blood to the sea until it washes away, something like that."

"Hm."

"I know."

"Maybe the river is your blood, and the morphine is what had to be diluted out. I've heard it can take a long time."

"Could be. It's strong stuff."

"Then again, the Vikings did eventually stop spilling the blood of the clergy. They turned Dublin into a major port, settled down, and stayed."

"That they did."

"So this was something you didn't want to tell me right away, in case I didn't like the idea of you braining a priest."

"Pretty much."

"It's sexy as hell," she said, digging into the kumi.

Chapter Thirty-nine

The Sun Temple, Konark, India, January 12, 2010

The sun temple was designed as a gigantic chariot, complete with enormous stone wheels. My instinct was to run up and touch it. I restrained myself.

It was a dry, breezy day with a few stray clouds, and we had an official academic guide, Bahswar, thanks to Keira's contacts in the shadowy network of degreed librarians.

"You can see, in the north niche, Surya, the sun god, is on a horse," he said. "This is rare for Indian iconography. In the west and south corners, Surya stands only. No horse."

Bahswar was young, tall, and thin, with a long, aquiline nose and a general air of contentment.

"The horse is the power to go north again?" said Keira.

"Perhaps," he said. "It is unknown. If Surya holds the reins, then it is Surya who stops the sun from dying, and turns the chariot north again. Surya is the power that bends the sun to its course."

"Like gravity," I said.

"Gravity is a great power," said Bahswar.

We moved on. Every part of the temple was covered with sculptured sandstone, including most every animal in the natural world. Around a corner, a smooth stone woman smiled, her hips to one side in a swaying dance. Closer up, I saw she wasn't all human.

"That mermaid is the most buxom of all the mermaids," I said.

"They are Nagas," said the always-pleasant Bahswar. "Shape-shifters. Guardians of treasure in the waters. They can appear human, and will marry kings and queens." The mermaid-Naga was playing a harp.

"Look at these two," said Keira. A tall, handsome man of stone had his arm around a beautiful woman, his elegantly sculpted left hand cupped around her lovely left breast.

"Cheeky," I said.

On another wall was a naked man reclining on a couch, with a naked woman on top, pulling herself to him with her arms around his shoulders. There were more embraces, in various convenient positions.

"When a man is in the embrace of his beloved spouse, he knows nothing as within and nothing as without," said Bahswar. "It is the union of male and female cosmic principles, Purusha and Shakti. People come here for their honeymoons." I wondered if I was staring too much.

"Purusha creates life outside of himself, through the light of consciousness," said Keira. "Shakti is the potential of life, she who creates within herself."

"You have been reading up," said Bahswar.

"It's a long flight from Dublin to Delhi."

We emerged from the stone orgy to a group of little people flying with various musical instruments.

"The gandharvas and apsaras are the musicians and the dancers that fly with the chariot," said Bahswar, having followed my gaze.

221

"What does the name Konark mean?" I asked.

"In Sanskrit, Konark is *sun in the southeast corner*," said Bahswar. "The day of the winter solstice. Right now, we are walking on the same path taken by the solstice sun."

We passed massive and intricately sculpted blocks of stone. As we walked, the path steadily narrowed until reaching a doorway with a stone elephant on either side. Bahswar gestured us inside. As my eyes got used to the lower light, Bahswar's voice echoed slightly.

"The audience chamber is Jagamohana. The arches are corbelled, and the roof is a pyramid shape."

We walked across the room, toward the inner sanctum, where the solstice sun would be narrowed further. It was empty except for a rectangular platform wide enough to lie down.

"The floor of the sanctum is ten meters on every side," said Bahswar. "It slopes to the north, where there is a drain. All the columns come out of sixteen-sided lotus flowers, which are dark green chlorite."

"The sun shines into the sanctum on the solstice," said Keira.

"Yes," said Bahswar. "I have been here several times. It is a humbling event."

"There was once a chlorite statue of Surya inside, embedded with gems that went missing," I said.

"Yes, long ago."

"When the sun struck the gems in the statue in the sanctum, they would refract the light, and send out beams of color," said Keira.

"Most certainly," said Bahswar.

Keira and I walked slowly around the audience chamber, taking in the intricate carving.

"Rama was married to Sita here," said Bahswar, his voice echoing slightly. "The joining of two royal families. The vases were filled with white and orange flowers, and the bride wore jewels in her hair and upon her dress. After the ceremony, they go into the inner sanctum, where Rama sees Sita for the first time, and they kiss."

A group of four walked inside, speaking in hushed tones.

Out in the sunlight, Bahswar lamented the condition of the temple, saying there was not enough money to prevent deterioration.

"I believe there will be more and more of the temple closed for public safety." He excused himself, saying he had to return to Odissa. We shook hands, Keira hugged him. I shook his hand a second time.

"You were kind to take the time for us," I said.

"Of course," said Bahswar.

As our guide departed, my mind went to our little cabin on the beach, just a half-mile from the temple. My provoked imagination was reeling off various possible adventures.

"I have a plan for this afternoon," said Keira.

"I was just thinking—"

"Not that plan."

"Oh."

"Trust me."

It was an hour before sunset when our long-tailed motorboat revved up and headed out into Chilika Lake.

"You're gonna like this," said Keira.

After ten minutes of parting the waters, the boat slowed. There were all sizes and colors of birds in the trees, on the water, and flying overhead. To our left, a pair of dolphins jumped from the lake. The engine purred quietly.

"They are the Irrawaddy dolphin," said Captain Subhudi. "It is the only population in India."

The same pair broke the water again, this time twice in a row. I scanned the lake for more dolphins. I saw something floating in the water, and pointed it out to the captain.

"Gill net," he said, maneuvering towards it. He pointed to a pole with a hook on it. The boat slowed. I leaned over the side with the pole and snared the net. Keira took a handful, and soon it was on the deck.

"They kill the dolphins," said the captain. "Once the Irrawaddy helped the fishermen. They drove the fish into their nets. They still do it far up the Ayeyawady River. Not here."

"How big is the lake?" I asked.

"Eleven hundred square kilometers. One hundred and thirty villages around it, and on the islands. It is the biggest winter ground for migrating birds in India."

I looked around. A snow-white egret was walking in shallow water by the shore. Keira handed me her binoculars. I scanned the shoreline.

"I see two, no, three flamingos. I see some ducks. And whoa, a bright blue and green bird."

"The Indian roller," said Captain Suhbudi.

I put down the binoculars.

"They really built the winter solstice temples on the winter grounds of migrating birds."

"I thought you'd like it," said Keira. "Brú na Bóinne is the winter ground of the whooper swan, the coast of Brittany and the mound at Carnac is one gigantic winter ground." Keira was counting off her fingers. "The Adriatic Flyway, from Central Europe to the Sudan, goes right down the Nile, and the Temple at Karnak, where there are lots and lots of migratory birds, including egrets and ibis, like here, where we have…"

"The Konark Sun Temple."

"Carnac is maybe 5,000 miles away, and it's at least six or seven thousand years old. Konark was built in the thirteenth century. That's a lot of space and time for a belief to stay true."

I looked through the binoculars again. The three flamingos were strutting through a marshy area by a small island.

"The birds carry the souls of the dead close to where the sun is dying too, in the southeast corner," said Captain Subhudi. "In this place, weakness and death become joy and strength."

I put the binoculars aside and knelt down on one knee in the boat, in front of Keira. I hadn't planned it this way, but it seemed like the right time, and the ring was in my pocket. The boat pitched slightly. I took out the box, and the ring. The colors of the rainbow glittered in the diamond.

"I thought you might do this," said Keira.

"I was planning it for later, but this seems like a nice spot."

"It's beautiful." A flock of chattering gulls flew past. "And there's a captain handy."

"Yes, there is." I was still kneeling, trying to keep my balance in the rolling boat.

"Like Sita and Rama," said Captain Subhudi. "I am happy to marry you."

"And we're already on the honeymoon," said Keira.

"Brilliant," I said, staying focused on not falling over sideways. "No worries."

"Except one." Keira looked at me and raised her feline eyebrows. "The words?"

Subhudi shut off the engine and the boat coasted forward.

"Will you marry me?"

A pair of Indian rollers flew by.

"I will."

I finally stood up, lurching to one side. Keira caught me. Captain Subhudi laughed.

"Very good," he said, turning the boat toward the closest island. "I will put down the anchor for the ceremony."

Chapter Forty

Cork City. September 14, 2010

"Nessa O'Dalaigh was born on the Beara—a rocky finger reaching into the Atlantic Ocean, where mist and fog are like members of the family…" I looked up from the index card. "Waddya think?"

"Startin' with a joke is always good," said Angus, the bartender at the Spit and Chatter Club, a few streets down from the exhibit hall at Cork City College.

"You think it's funny?"

Angus leaned on the bar and looked out the wide front windows. "It's a little bit funny, but you don't want to start off with a big joke anyway, do ya?"

"No."

"Just right then."

I figured a slow pint of Guinness was needed before my brief speech at the opening of the exhibit. I was more proud of Nessa than I was of me finding her, and I was happy enough with that. I lifted a glass to her work, and her new life out of time.

Angus drifted back down the bar. There was a couple at the other end, nuzzling in the afternoon.

"So you sold the letters, the bits of old manuscript, the…"

"The sixteen millimeter film from Iceland, and the primer."

"To help build yourself a house on the family land."

"Right."

"And it's all at a new exhibit up the road."

"Hundredth anniversary of the Celtic Revival."

"I'll have to stop in after the shift. Another pint?" The glass
was near empty.

"No, thanks. I'll need control of my tongue later." I finished
the Guinness and left a small pile of euros on the bar. "Nice
meetin' ya, Angus. Thanks for yer ears."

"Not too funny now," he said. The door jingled behind me.

A light mist was blowing in from the east, from the Irish Sea.
I zipped my jacket and started walking. It had been a long time
since I'd spoken in public. It was back on the Cape, moderating a
candidate's debate the night before an election for the board of
selectmen.

Now, I waited in a room next to the Puxley Exhibition Hall. A
poster lying on the desk read "A Window on the Celtic Revival:
100 Years Later." In the background was a sun, half-risen from the
horizon—the Irish battle flag of Finn Mac Cool.

From behind the curtain, I saw Keira in the front row. *Just
look at me if you get stuck.* Hearing my name, I walked to the dais.
I didn't know there'd be a microphone there. A low buzz came
from the speakers. I arranged my three by five cards, and was
about to speak when the mic made a popping noise, then emitted a
little shriek. I felt a surge of adrenalin in my chest and arms. I
found the switch for the microphone and turned it off. I looked at
Keira, my consort, and looked down at my gold ring.

"Nessa was the name of an Irish queen, mother of Conor Mac
Nessa," My voice sounded loud, but steady. "Nessa O Dalaigh was
born on the Beara in West Cork, three hundred years after the last
rebels and holdouts in Ireland cursed in Gaelic at Cromwell and his
men, before dyin' for the cause."

I paused for a moment.

"But only ten years later, the children of Cromwell's army spoke Gaelic, and went to Irish pubs and listened to Irish music, and their children did the same. It's been that way since the Tuatha Dé Danann disappeared into the mounds and under the waters to the Other World, knowin' full well that to reign over the Other World is to reign over this one.

"So, Nessa is here today, tellin' us what she wished to say a hundred years ago. That the Irish soul is always whisperin' in the waters, tellin' its story again, so wade into the waves, still your mind and listen closely…"

The Flight of Souls:
Vessels and Mechanisms

This document was transcribed from the journal found in Nessa Harrington's burial place. It appears to be a compendium of acquired knowledge on the esoteric subject of soul travel. The note and quotation below were written on the inside page.

"When the song men hymn the god in their own art, and the harpists are twangling a harmonious accompaniment, the swans make their concordant music, not losing time or tune, as though they had got the keynote from the choir conductor, and were joining their natural music with that of the artists of the sacred minstrelsy; and then, when the hymn, ends, away they fly… "

– Diodorus Siculus, writing of a concert of swans and men given for the sun god Apollo on the spring equinox on the mysterious island of Hyperborea in the far north.

The soul between lifetimes

There are numerous questions regarding the period between two lifetimes. Where does the soul go? How does it travel? Does it require some kind of container? Do all souls complete the process of reincarnation and return for another life? If not, where do they go, and what happens to them? In the face of such ponderous unknowns, a useful first step is to examine various circumstances in which we find the soul traveling between lifetimes in pre-Christian stories and texts.

Soul in the tree

An ancient Irish tale tells of a wicked specter that tricks a young couple into believing the other has died. Consumed by the grief of young love, they each commit suicide, unaware of the depth of their own tragedy. They are buried side by side, and over the years, a yew tree grows at the head of the man's grave, and an apple tree by the woman's. It becomes plain for visitors to see the likeness of the woman in the apple tree, and the man's face in the yew.

Believing the trees were magical, the druids cut them down to make wooden tablets, upon which they wrote vision-tales of young love to perform at the Feast of Samain. After hearing the poems, the king was in awe, and asked for the magic tablets. As he held them in wonder, they sprang together and were joined fast; impossible to part. They are kept in the treasury of Tara. An alternate version describes the likenesses of the young lovers in the two trees, which grew together above the two graves, entangled as one, never to be parted.

Soul in the stone

Stones of every size, color, and type have been carved, etched, and painted to attract ancestral souls to take up residence inside them during important annual festivals. A ring of standing stones receives the most highly celebrated ancestors, so the people might learn from their divine qualities. The ancestors in the stones enjoy seeing the ritual feast performed with timeless art. As markers in the landscape that align with the moon, sun, and stars, the standing stones and their resident ancestral souls are immoveable guideposts to the universe, showing the way to immortality.

Men would chase their wives around the great stones at night, finally engaging in intercourse, hoping the celebrated ancestral soul would inhabit their child. Despite Christian laws that forbade the practice in the Medieval period, men still chased their naked wives around dolmens on a full moon—the white orb brimming with refreshed souls.

Soul in the clouds, moon, and stars

Like a river on earth, the ascending river of souls has "boats" going in both directions—towards the place of rest and rejuvenation, and back to earth for the next incarnation.

In some cases, the journey begins with cremation of the dead, intended to lift the soul in smoke to join the clouds, which float past the horizon and beyond the edge of this world, drifting on to the moon and stars.

Star maps painted on the ceilings in hundreds of Egyptian tombs show the Milky Way leading north to the imperishable stars, forever circling around the northern celestial pole.

The destination of martyred souls

The "imperishable" star never falls below the horizon, always visibly circling the celestial pole. These ircumpolar stars were the eternal destination for those who sacrificed their lives to save others—those who need not return for another incarnation.

The Vedic poet Dadhicha is among the imperishable stars, having agreed to death so his bones could be made into a magical weapon for Lord Indra to defeat Vrtra, the water-hoarding dragon. "And those brilliant regions that are seen from the earth in the form of stars...blazing with splendor all their own. And there he beheld (those) who had yielded up their lives...stationed in their respective places."– *Mahabharata: Section XLII, Indralokagamana Parva*

The Egyptian Pyramid Texts say, "...may you lift me and raise me to the Winding Waterway, may you set me among the gods, the Imperishable stars...the White Palace of the great ones..." W.B. Yeats draws on similar imagery in *A Dialogue of Self and Soul.*

My Soul I summon to the winding ancient stair; [SEP]
Set all your mind upon the steep ascent, [SEP]
Upon the broken, crumbling battlement, [SEP]
Upon the breathless starlit air,
Upon the star that marks the hidden pole;
Fix every wandering thought upon [SEP]
That quarter where all thought is done.

Place of rest for those returning

Time is the measure of cyclical change; it counts off the wearing down of all things. The destination of souls who must rest and rejuvenate is the northern celestial pole; the immoveable pivot point around which everything turns.

The fourth century Welsh druid and poet Taliesin described the celestial pole as "the pin of pivotal space," located "above the breastwork of the High River mouth," (at the northern end of the Milky Way).

It is the only part of the sky that never moves, and thus immune from the turning of time around it. A place of timelessness has no cause and effect, no consequences are due. In Tír na nÓg, the joy and play of youth returns.

Taliesin describes the nine stars that turn closest around the celestial pole as angelic maidens helping souls to rejuvenate, writing that, "...nine maidens kindle the cauldron by their breathing." The *'cauldron'* described the celestial pole, and all that turned around it, as one stirs a cauldron. In Hindu legend, it is the Churning Ocean of Milk.

Souls returning

Once the soul is cleansed, rested and rejuvenated, it desires to manifest again, and animate a new form. The earliest stargazers placed this moment at the winter solstice, when the Ursid meteor shower falls from the celestial pole. Five or ten meteors per hour can be seen, but there are bursts of greater numbers.

Taliesin wrote of a fountain originating from a "turning fortress" in the northern sky, known as *caer siddi*. "My song sounded in the four-towered Caer, forever turning...I have been three times resident in the castle of Arianrhod (the moon)."

For the Hindu, the returning souls float down the Milky Way "as braided locks in waves 'til the orb of the moon grows bright from the misty crystal current." [*Vishnu Purana*] After the full moon, the souls-in-water fall from the moon to the summit of Mt. Meru. In spring's melt water, the great rivers of India run with souls ready to manifest.

In Celtic tradition, becoming pregnant is more likely five days after a full moon, when new souls have had a chance to descend to the clouds, and fall to earth in rain or snow. In Germanic culture, souls waited to reincarnate in "baby pools" or wells.

Special souls often descend on a cloud. Queen Maya of Nepal dreamed that a small white elephant descended on a cloud and

233

circled her three times before entering her side. She was pregnant, and her son would become the Buddha.

Crystal bridges

It was so desirable for one's soul to successfully navigate the cosmic loop of reincarnation, a variety of methods were used to establish some sort of connection between the earthly realm and the starry night sky, some means of guaranteed passage from one to the other.

The Nature Religions considered rock crystals to be the highest form of water—containers of seed-souls that carried them to earth from the celestial pole. Temples were often covered or topped with white quartz, including Bru na Bouinne, and the Great Pyramid's capstone.

Both stars and quartz crystal are white and sparkling, yet also refract colors. Clear crystal and water are both transparent and reflective. Perhaps the warmth of the sun turns the star-crystals into snow, clouds and rain. But some fall directly to earth. Thus, heating rock crystal and creating steam could release immortal soul.

Taliesin identified crystal as a form of water when he wrote of the three fountains of the celestial pole, which were: the source of rain, the source of seawater, and "the third is in the vein of the mountains, like a sparkling feast.

Turn above, Turn below

An essential element of creating a spirit-connection between earth and the celestial pole was to walk or dance in a circle around a temple such as Brú na Bóinne, mimicking the constant turning of the heavens around the fountain of life at the celestial pole. In the Celtic legend of Boann, she circles the mythical/celestial Well of Sergais three times, causing pure waters to burst forth, creating the River Boinne.

The little people dressed in white and dancing in a circle appear at night in the Irish countryside. If they invite you to dance, you are warned not to miss a step. The connection must be maintained.

In a popular Hindu legend, the gods use a giant snake to turn Mount Mandara like a spinning top, thereby "churning the ocean of milk" (the turning stars), from which comes jewels, sacred animals, a physician and the nectar of immortality.

Walking around temples, mountains, wells and new homes is a near-universal practice known as circumambulation, once intended to activate a sacred connection with the celestial pole.

Immoveable above, Immoveable below

A foundational quality of the celestial pole is that it never moves. In order to establish a connection with the celestial pole, something immoveable must be constructed on earth.

This is a primary reason for the sheer size of standing stones and ancient temples—to assure they were immoveable, and therefore would forever retain their connection to the pole. The stone basin in the central chamber at Dowth is wider than the two passages leading out of the mound. It can never be moved.

Timeless above, Timeless below

Another important element of establishing a connection between below and above is to match the timelessness of Tír na nÓg with timelessness on earth. In the central chamber at Brú na Bóinne, timeless experiences included steaming, fasting and the deprivation of the senses, which can result in "visions."

Music from the Dagda's harp in the acoustically resounding central chamber was doubtless a timeless experience, and there was just enough room for two to dance. The timeless experiences of marriage and death were surely celebrated in ancient temples, accompanied by music.

The all-night circling dance may be the oldest method to conjur up a sense of timelessness, as displayed now and again on moonlit nights in the countryside by the little people dressed in white.

The goal of musicians, poets and playwrights is to construct timeless art performed on a center stage, lifting the spirits of the surrounding audience, leaving the mundane world behind.

Spiral travel

The soul's travel to the timeless celestial pole was symbolized in the spiral, found all over Brú na Bóinne, and other sacred places. It was obvious enough that turning a stick in shallow water will pull sand and silt upwards from the bottom, like a dust-devil, tornado or waterspout.

Scottish legends tell of people taken up by a whirlwind to a pleasant journey across the sky, and returning home safely by morning. Yet the spiral did not mean to ascend, as numerous legends mention a famous whirlpool in the Irish Sea.

The spiral was a symbol for transport, from this world to the Other World, thus the appearance of spirals etched on the stones of the central chamber at Bru na Boinne, as the walls of a cave were taken to be a membrane between the worlds.

Nuts of Knowledge

The unalterable Truth shares the unchanging quality of the celestial pole, meaning Tír na nÓg is not only a place of rest and pleasure, but of eternal Truth.

In Celtic legends, the heated quartz crystals that produce steam are symbolized as "Nuts of Knowledge" dropped into a stream. The spiral etchings and triangles on the Entrance Stone reflect the Celtic fondness for overlapping meanings. The triangles signify quartz crystals radiating heat, while the spirals signify both "up-lifting" and "steam," indicating the elevating effects to be found in the temple of Brú na Bóinne.

The Entrance Stone must have been all the more compelling when it was in the center of a shallow pool near the entrance to the mound, the spirals seemingly rising from the waterline of the shallow pool, which itself was likely stocked with heated quartz stones.

Retaining and radiating heat

Born of heat and water, it appears the soul requires some amount of warmth to survive. The soul may reside in water, stones or trees, all of which retain heat in a way that is plain to deduce. Any crystal retains and radiates heat more effectively than other kinds of stone, and was thus was a preferred container for the soul.

The soul spends most of its time inside a warm body, which it puts to work finding external sources of warmth to guarantee survival. Inside its body, the soul resides in the warm blood. The dying body grows colder as the soul gathers its warmth.

In the billowing smoke of cremation the soul reaches the clouds and flies beyond the horizon. The soul may travel contained in the warmth of moonbeams and starlight. The souls may be transported in the heat and joy of music. The harmonizing choir at a funeral creates a vessel of music to lift and heal the soul.

Musical poetry and the Whooper Swan

Among the oldest practices of the Nature Religion is singing, chanting, or otherwise making music during funerary ceremonies. Egyptian priests sang specific verses to aid the ascension of the soul.

The soul can be contained in the warm poetry of song, embraced among the notes. The more artful the song, the more elegant the verse...the higher the warming soul may rise.

The Celtic Dagda had his harp when he arrived from Fairyland to make his home at Brú na Bóinne, where birds sang in trees of purple crystal. The Hindu river goddess Saraswati played a string instrument as she flew down to earth on a swan, holding a pot of water and crystals. The Hindu gandharvas were celestial musicians.

The whooper swan is known to fly at impossible heights, barely observable by the naked eye, yet observers can hear the sound of their constant calling. It is their music-making that ties the flock together during their long journey.

Early Icelanders believed the whoopers were super-natural, and made annual journeys to their ancestral home in Valhalla. During their winter absence, northern people could see the stars of Cygnus, the swan, steadily fly around the northern celestial pole, until in the spring the lowest stars of Cygnus drops below the horizon, just as the whoopers returned to prepare their giant nests for the year's young.

The Story of the Imazegan

This is the story told by Ogma to Danu at the mounds of the Boyne Valley in the distant past. After Danu told of her people following musical swans from the north, Ogma laughed so hard he began to cough. His story would be much the same ...

In the beginning, when the ice-mountains melted and flooded the valley, our people fled to the high desert. After weeks of heavy rain, a great shallow lake had formed in the great expanse of sand.

When the sun finally returned, the people ran into the water, drinking and splashing each other. They laughed and smiled in happiness and thanks. As the sun went down that day, dozens of great birds came from the clouds, each white wing the size of a man.

The people stood frozen in place, watching the great birds descend, circling the lake three times. With their wings held wide to slow them, their webbed feet split the waters and they glided to a stop.

It was the largest flying bird they had seen. In the water, the birds used their long necks like a snake to pull plants from below. That night, the people gathered along the shore and listened to their echoing calls and soft conversation.

It is said that two hunters approached the birds that first night with slings and stones, but an alarm of honks awoke the flock, which rushed together at the hunters in a flurry of bony wings and jabbing beaks. From that day forward, they were not to be closely approached. The great birds had earned their new home.

Inspired by the unusual events, a Society of Watchers formed. Sitting on the hillsides around the lake, they wore white-feather cloaks and white feathers in their hair. They named the creature Zegan. It meant *free of bonds; without boundary*. They kept a book to record the bird's behavior, their arrivals in the fall and their departures in spring.

Each fall, they led the celebrations of the flock's return with drinks of fermented fruit, roasted mountain goat, drumming and dancing. The Watchers saw that the non-breeding Zegans always arrived first, and cleared the winter grounds by rushing in groups at the other creatures on the lakeshore. When the extended families arrived, there was a long and elaborate greeting of calls back and forth. The next day, the non-breeders flew together up the valley to shallow mountain lakes, where they steamed in hot springs and played at contests through the winter. The families remained, feeding in the great shallow lake, and the marshes around it.

In time, the Watchers learned that a single Zegan couple produced more than a dozen generations of young, and stayed together as long as they lived. They accepted orphans as their own. The Watchers came to believe the birds had been sent as models of peace and prosperity, and eventually, the village accepted a new way to live. Every person would become a breeder, join the *Watchers*, or join the *Fiagan*. There were simple rules.

Make respectful greetings to all after time away.
Resolve grievances by contests.
The *Fiagan* never interfere with families.
The *Fiagan* help and protect the flock.
The Watchers judge disputes, and set the course.

Then the storms stopped coming. Without the clouds to catch them, the rays of the merciless sun shrank the lake a little more each year. The marshes grew smaller, and the grasses withered. Fewer Zegans returned in winter. One spring, before the Zegans flew away to the northwest, to their mysterious summer home, the Watchers invited the people to follow them, to find greater prosperity. Some stayed and dug deeper for water, but most followed; bringing dried fish and fruits, nuts, sorghum and blankets.

As the few remaining Zegans flew northwest from the shrunken lake that spring, so did two hundred of our ancestors, along with their goats and goods. At first, the people moved quickly northward through high valleys, always keeping the river in sight. But after a few days the river turned east and the route of the Zegans was northwest, across an unknown desert. It was an act of faith to leave the green valleys behind.

Descending into a desert of black rocks and yellow sand, they walked at night for weeks, keeping the cold away with their movement, and conserving their food and water. As the food ran out, they took lizards and snakes with their slingshots. Then the water ran out.

The desert stretched on, and after two days, the people grew weak. They could not aim their slingshots and so they dug a few sleeping lizards from their holes. The next night, some could not walk, and two of the oldest died in the cold, just before dawn. That day, the strongest man and woman went ahead, leaving the rest in the shade of a rock outcropping.

That night the man and woman returned, having discovered a series of caves in a sandstone hillside. In one of the caves was a small spring. Our people used their last strength to walk through the long, cold night, stumbling and huddled in blankets. When they arrived, they drank from the spring, and made a fire at the mouth of the cave.

In the first glowing light of day, the sun rose over the hillside to the southeast, casting a beam through a split in the dark rock, so it fell upon an outcrop of white crystal just inside the cave. The bright sun caused the rock crystal to glow in red and yellow colors, then green and blue. The colored light brightened the walls of the cave. Weak with hunger and ecstatic with joy, our people took comfort. They would live.

Inside the cave, they took out their most valuable possessions. The Book of Zegan Records, of which there were three volumes, containing all the observations of the Watchers, and a record of the Zegan families going back many generations. The books were made of goat-skin, and the people were starving. Before this last meal, they read each book aloud from beginning to end in the dark of the cave.

Setting out in the morning, they were visited with shading clouds and a cooling light rain. The next morning, they saw a flock of brown birds, and came upon a wide river. They drank and bathed, and built fish traps. They followed the river for three days until they came upon a small flock of Zegans among the marshy islands of a river mouth. The river emptied into a vast sea.

The people who made this journey were the first Imazegan. They took the name that day, when they found the flock. To be Imazegan meant to be free of bonds, to be a people without boundaries.

After crossing the desert and making their new home along the sea coast, the Imazegan wrote again the Book of Zegan from their memories, and began new record-keeping. In early winter, a dozen Zegan families flew in from the northwest, and spent the winter with the smaller flock. In the spring, most of the Zegans flew northwest across the open sea, while a small group stayed at the river mouth.

Over generations, the Imazegan learned to build boats and became expert fishermen, spreading west along the coast, growing more populous and more skilled on the ocean. They talked across the waters with drums of all sizes, made from the trunks of the sycamore tied over with goatskin. But the heat that chased them from the high desert also found them along the sea. The burning sun dried up the marshlands and shrank the rivers. Again, fewer and fewer of the sacred birds returned each year. Soon the Imazegan would follow them if they wished to survive.

Through one summer, fall and winter, the Imazegan built twelve sailing vessels, and in the spring they followed the Zegan northwest across the unknown ocean. Under fair breezes for one day and most of a night, they sailed with a group of curious whales, and were followed by hundreds of circling seabirds.

In the moonlit night, they saw an island in the distance, but upon rowing closer, the leading boat was tossed by a current onto a knife-edged rock that pierced and sunk the craft. With sea-birds shrieking in the dark and sharks in the water, two were lost and fifteen saved.

At first light, the wind died away and the boats floated gently in the water. The Imazegan drummed and sang all morning, to lift the spirits of their lost people to the clouds. Freeing their boats from the shoals, they sang all through the windless day to the rhythm of the oars, pulling northwest with every muscle, until in the cool dusk, a long shoreline appeared.

In the morning they found Zegan nests along the mouth of a river, and still more further inland. They were empty. The summer grounds were still further. The Imazegan left their boats in the forest near the shore, and walked northwest into a maze of deep valleys, winding rivers and sloping hills covered in forests of maple, oak and chestnut. They lived on fish, fruits and nuts, zig-zagging over ridges and down canyons to best stay their determined northwest course.

By mid-summer, they came to the head of a tidal river that led to another sea, this one colder than the last. They followed the coastline northwest for a day, and into the night, until they came upon dozens of Zegan nests. They had been here over the past winter. They were still further north, but they would return.

The Imazegan gathered stones and heated them in a fire-pit on the beach. With stag's antlers they took the stones from the fire and spaced them to make a great circle in the sand. Walking the circle, they whipped wet branches over each stone, causing steam to rise until the circle was closed.

Deep into the cold night, they drummed and danced inside the circle of steam, their ceremonial wings casting long shadows on the beach.

Afterword

Every effort was made to be historically accurate in both the letters and flashbacks contained in *People of the Flow*. The descriptions of the Easter Rising in May 1916 came from the notes of journalists that were conpiled years later by *The Irish Times*.

Chapter 14 contains excerpts of an interview between author W.Y. Evans-Wentz and the Seer of Bohernabreena, as first published in *The Fairy Faith in Celtic Countries*, in 1911. Chapter 25 contains excerpts of the mythic dialogue between St. Patrick and Oisin, taken from *A Literary History of Ireland: From Earliest Times to the Present Day*, by Douglas Hyde.

The historical figures in *People of the Flow* are, in order of appearance: Agnes O'Farrelly, scholar and member of the Board of Governors at Dublin University College; the romantic poet George Russell; dramatist and theater manager Lady Gregory; and Douglas Hyde, linguist and scholar.

]Dr. Strange and the Strangelies was a Dublin-based folk/rock band in the late 1960s and early '70s, which occasionally gets together again for a gig in Castletownbere.